# HOW TO CAPTURE AN INVISIBLE CAT

# THE GENIUS FACTOR

# HOW TO CAPTURE AN INVISIBLE CAT

## Paul Tobin

illustrated by
## Thierry Lafontaine

BLOOMSBURY

NEW YORK  LONDON  OXFORD  NEW DELHI  SYDNEY

First published in the United States of America in March 2016
by Bloomsbury Children's Books
www.bloomsbury.com

Bloomsbury is a registered trademark of Bloomsbury Publishing Plc

For information about permission to reproduce selections from this book, write to
Permissions, Bloomsbury Children's Books, 1385 Broadway, New York, New York 10018
Bloomsbury books may be purchased for business or promotional use. For information on
bulk purchases please contact Macmillan Corporate and Premium Sales Department at
specialmarkets@macmillan.com

Library of Congress Cataloging-in-Publication Data
Tobin, Paul.
The genius factor : how to capture an invisible cat / by Paul Tobin ;
illustrated by Thierry Lafontaine.
pages      cm
Summary: Socially awkward fifth-grade genius Nate Bannister recruits
his classmate Delphine to help him reverse one of his many experiments
(a dinosaur-sized invisible cat) while foiling the schemes of the world's
most dastardly organization, the Red Death Tea Society.
ISBN 978-1-61963-840-2 (hardcover)  •  ISBN 978-1-61963-841-9 (e-book)
[1. Adventure and adventurers—Fiction. 2. Science—Experiments—Fiction.
3. Genius—Fiction. 4. Humorous stories.] I. Lafontaine, Thierry, illustrator.
II. Title. III. Title: How to capture an invisible cat.
PZ7.T5617Fr 2016        [Fic]—dc23        2015008383

Book design by John Candell
Typeset by RefineCatch Limited, Bungay, Suffolk
Printed and bound in USA by Berryville Graphics, Berryville, Virginia
2  4  6  8  10  9  7  5  3  1

**For Colleen**

# HOW TO CAPTURE AN INVISIBLE CAT

chapter
1

Let's just say the cat was bigger than a horse.

To be honest, the cat was nearly the size of an elephant, but that sounds too scary, so . . . let's just say the cat was bigger than a horse.

It had claws the size of my fingers.

It had teeth the length of my forearm.

It was hissing so forcefully that my hair was blowing in the wind of its breath.

Its name was Proton.

It was invisible, odorless, and silent.

It was trying to kill me.

It was Nate's fault.

I should probably explain.

Nate's smart. That's for sure.

His IQ had been measured by amateurs, who returned results that made eyes pop wide. These results had been checked and rechecked and submitted to experts, who rushed to Polt Middle School to investigate Nathan Bannister with further and far more difficult tests.

These tests took place a couple of weeks back, after school, in our sixth grade classroom. I'd stayed late to sweep the floor, since Ms. Talbot uses cleaning duty as a punishment for misbehaving children, among which I am numbered. Nate was there, blinking at these experts, these men and women who'd come to Polt from as near as Portland and as far away as New York, London, and a city in Russia that had a name far past my ability to pronounce. Nate was blinking at these Very Serious People, not understanding why they were giving him such simple tests. The chalkboards were covered with Nate's equations, equations that were making the experts shiver. There were three women dressed in skirts and cardigans, and a man in a horrible green suit. He was muttering to himself and leaned up against the blackboard, getting chalk on his suit from where Ms. Talbot's weekly cleaning duty list was posted, which at the time happened to have my name, Delphine, written five times in a row.

I was fascinated, and it wasn't because of the dreadful green suit or my name on the chalkboard, but because my classmate, Nate, a boy I'd never really paid any attention to, was pointing out the mistakes in *their* math, and suddenly it felt like *they* were the ones being tested. And they were failing.

I let out a little laugh.

Nate looked over to me.

He smiled.

I smiled back.

And then I went back to pushing the broom.

That was the first day that I really started to pay attention to Nate. I wanted to know why so many people had come from so far to meet him, even though most everyone in our middle school barely noticed him, myself included. It wasn't until later that we became friends, and that his invisible cat almost killed me. Sort of. It's a long story that starts with dogs.

Nate has a Scottish terrier named Bosper, and I walk dogs as a part-time job. It takes up a lot of time, three days a week after school, but it earns me enough money to buy comic books and fund my weekly Cake vs. Pie meetings, which are a never-ending debate between me and my friends, despite the obvious superiority of cake. Plus, I have to pay for my cell phone by myself, and I'm also saving up for when my friend Liz Morris and I start traveling the world as a mysterious duo of carefree adventurers. Sadly, from the looks of my savings, that will probably have to wait until at least seventh grade.

Anyway, Nate and I were both at the Mark Twain Memorial Dog Park. He had Bosper, and I was surrounded by an assortment of dogs ranging from wiener dogs to Saint Bernards, all of them in the mood to bark and drool and twist their leashes around my legs.

There was a young girl at the dog park, maybe five years old, playing with a blue balloon. She was having the time of her life. But of course she lost her grip on the balloon and it soared right up into the air and began floating away.

"Ahhhh!" the girl yelled. She crumpled to the grass, devastated.

"I'll get it!" I said, despite the fact that at four feet seven inches I'm not exactly the most excellent height for grabbing runaway balloons.

I hurriedly tied my dogs to a statue of a swan, and then spent the next thirty seconds in a humiliating attempt to grab the balloon. It kept dancing in the air just out of my reach, which made my desperate grabs all the more idiotic. At one point it looked like it was going to get caught in a tree so I climbed up into the branches, providing me an excellent view of the balloon floating far away.

"Bosper!" I heard somebody yell. I looked down from my perch in the tree and saw Nate Bannister with his flopping brown hair and that nose that's too big, and his glasses and the checkered shirt along with the pants where, if you look closely enough, you'll see several equations. In pen.

Nate has brown eyes, and the wind was blowing softly. Not that I mean to connect these two facts in any particular way.

"Fetch that balloon!" Nate ordered his dog, which was ridiculous. Why did Nate think his dog could fetch the balloon when I couldn't? I mean, I'm not tall, but I'm way taller than a terrier.

The dog bounded off.

I climbed out of the tree.

Nate sat on a bench and went back to reading.

The dog was going the wrong way.

I told Nate, "Your dog's going the wrong way."

He looked up at me with a smile and said, "Wait for it," which I've grown to understand is one of his key phrases.

So I waited for it. I watched Bosper run across the dog park, completely in the opposite direction of where the balloon was going, running right past the poor screaming girl who had lost her balloon and who was now on her back rolling all over the ground, which is not something I'd recommend in a dog park. After a bit, the balloon went higher into the skies and then . . . and *then* it hit some wind currents and changed direction five or six times and eventually floated to a spot only two feet off the ground, right where Bosper was waiting for it. The dog calmly took the string in his mouth and trotted over to the girl, where he handed off the balloon and then flopped down at Nate's side to chew on a stick in a casual manner that suggested nothing marvelous had just happened.

But it had.

"What the piffle?" I said, amazed at what I'd seen. "How'd he do that?" ("Piffle," incidentally, is a word I use so that I don't get into trouble with Mom. I would be in trouble if she understood my definition for the word.)

"Air currents," Nate said. "Simply a matter of tracking them. Judging them. The connections. Chaos theory. Fractals. Quantum projections. Combining these factors."

"Simple," I said. It was not what I meant. I noticed he was reading a Nancy Drew mystery. I liked him for that. Most boys don't like girl detectives.

"Of course it's simple," Nate said. I don't think he meant it, either. I think he was testing me.

I said, "I lied. I have no idea what you're talking about."

"I didn't think so. Most people don't. I guess I'm smarter than most people." He sounded sad. He sounded lonely. I felt bad for him. I've always had about a million friends. I'm not ever lonely. But I guess I know what lonely looks like and sounds like. I'm smart enough for that.

I sat down on the bench, smoothed out my clothes, and took off my hat. I put out my hand to shake.

I said, "I'm Delphine Cooper."

"Nate Bannister. Most people call me Egghead."

"I'm not going to."

"Okay." He sounded happy about that.

I said, "So, obviously you're smart. But, how did your dog know where to wait for the balloon?"

"His name is Bosper."

"I got that part."

"He figured it out for himself."

"You lost me there."

Nate said, "Don't tell anyone this." He stopped and looked around to make sure we couldn't be overheard. I leaned in, acutely aware that we were so close and so very much in public that I could be starting rumors about me and Nate. But I wanted to hear.

"I accelerated him," Nate said. That . . . didn't mean anything to me. I looked down to Bosper. He didn't look any faster than a regular dog.

I said, "I, um . . ."

"I made his brain work a bit better. He does calculations."

"Stick," said Bosper, chewing on his stick.

I lost my breath. I flopped back on the bench, heaving.

Nate said, "So, you heard him?"

"Ye-ye-ye-yeah," I said.

"Bosper!" Bosper said.

Nate said, "When I accelerated him, he learned to talk. He's not very good at it."

8

"Not very good at it!" Bosper said, happily.

Nate said, "His tongue's not optimized for speaking. Our own mouths and tongues have been shaped for speech by evolution."

"Bosper has a bad mouth!" the dog said.

"We're in the park, Bosper," Nate said. He gave a nod and a raised eyebrow, keeping his hands on his Nancy Drew book but pointing all around the dog park with a finger. The terrier slunk low, returning to his stick. I was close to passing out. It still hadn't occurred to me to breathe.

"Bosper is bad," the dog said.

"He's not supposed to talk in public," Nate explained.

"He's not supposed to talk at *all*," I answered. My words sounded like a snake being stepped on. I was really going to have to start breathing. I honestly and truly was. Breathing is, like, the dumbest habit to give up.

"He's usually quiet around other people," Nate murmured. His eyes had gone distant, and his thumbs were twitching. He wasn't talking to me anymore. As I got to know Nate, I found out that about half the time he's not talking to me; he's only pondering genius thoughts. And then about twenty percent of the time he talks over my head. The rest of the time he's okay.

"*Why* is he talking?" Nate mused. He'd stood. He was pacing. He was tapping his forehead with a finger. He

9

looked to the sky, then the ground, then to me. He said, "Delphine, you really should breathe."

I did.

The world quit swimming quite so badly, and I didn't feel like passing out anymore. I *did* feel like I wanted a whole bunch of answers. Of course, when it comes to Nate, having the answers and *understanding* those answers are two completely separate issues.

"Nose!" Nate said. Kind of loud, really. I jumped.

"Nose?" I asked.

"Exactly!" Nate said. His finger came out to touch my nose. "There are five million scent receptors in there," he told me.

"In here?" I said. I held my nose in case my scent receptors were going to fall out. I mean, five million of them? That would make a horrible mess.

"But over here," Nate said, touching the terrier's nose, "are one hundred and forty-seven million scent receptors."

"That's thirty times more!" I said. I was hoping he'd be impressed with my math. Somebody should be, sometime, right?

"Twenty-nine point four," Nate corrected. "Well, by pure math, that is. But in reality it's many times more than that. For one thing, his brain contains forty times the scent processing power of our own, multiplying his progression arc."

"My brain's hurting here, Nate."

"I'm saying his sense of smell is at least ten thousand times better than ours."

"Ewww," I said, immediately thinking of how bad my brother Steve's gym clothes would reek to Bosper.

"I know this looks silly," Nate said.

"What does?" I asked. But by the time I spoke Nate had reached into a canvas messenger bag with sewn-on patches of Isaac Newton, Nikola Tesla, Albert Einstein, and the Muppet guy . . . Jim Henson, and he'd pulled out a mechanical dog nose. It had a strap that Nate put around his head. The nose went over his own. The mechanical nose made a whirring sound. And a snorting sound.

"That definitely looks silly," I said.

"It lets me smell like a dog." He began making adjustments.

"Bosper!" Bosper said.

Nate picked up my arm and smelled it.

"Oh!" he said. "That scent!"

"Piffle!" I said, yanking my arm back. "Why did you do that?"

"Delphine!" Bosper said. This was the first time I ever heard a dog say my name. It was unsettling, but also . . . *amazing.*

"We're going to be friends," Nate said, with a look of awe on his dog-nosed face. "I get it now! That's why Bosper was talking to you! Because he already knew! Good boy!" Nate leaned down and patted the terrier's head. Bosper reacted by jumping up and down in a circle, excited past any ability to control.

"Nobody here knows what you're talking about," I told Nate, which wasn't exactly true. Bosper clearly understood. Meaning a dog was one up on me.

"Your scent," Nate said, holding out his hand to shake. "You smell like a friend."

"What?" I said. I can't say I expected an answer. The trends so far hadn't been good.

"I'm going to have a friend," Nate said. He was so happy that I was afraid he was going to jump up and down like Bosper. I was also afraid that he'd never take that nose off.

Anyway, that's how Nathan Bannister and I became friends.

"I'm home!" I said, and picked up the lint brush that I always keep on the table just inside the door. If there were a list of things that dog hair clings to, the primary item on that list would be me, Delphine Cooper, as I am apparently made of glue.

"In here," Mom said from her office, which is just off our dining room. I walked inside and she had six million papers (my best guess, though there might have been seven million) spread all over her desk. On these papers were the complaints and demands of about thirty artists and musicians. Mom's job is finding galleries and gigs for them, helping sell their work, and so on. She thinks the artists are more consistently crazy, but the musicians are more intensely insane.

"Hey, Mom," I said. "Still working?"

"I should be done in a decade," she said, waving a couple of pieces of paper at me. "Apparently, a rat appeared at the Floating World gallery opening last night."

"Ick. And the artist was mad?"

"Just the opposite. She was thrilled. She said a frightened crowd is more likely to buy art. She sold ten paintings last night and now she wants me to set rats free at *all* her openings. Do you know how many permits you have to get in order to let wild animals free at public events?"

"No," I said. "I do not. Where's Dad?"

"He drove Steve out to the mall, because Steve's sister drew little cartoon animals on most of his T-shirts."

"Steve's sister," I said. "That would be me."

"That would be you," Mom agreed. There might have been a scowl involved, but it was difficult to tell, because of all the glares and grimaces. I thought about telling Mom that I'd only drawn on Steve's shirts because of how he'd filled my favorite sneakers full of potato salad, but then she might wonder *why* he'd done that, and I would have to confess certain things that I felt no need to make public.

"Will they be back in time for supper?" I asked, because I was a bit hungry, and because it was time to steer the topic away from me being in trouble, or any possible questions about why I'd spent twenty-four dollars on shaving cream and covered Steve's bedroom floor in nearly three feet of it, which is something I was hoping Mom didn't know.

"Don't think so," Mom said. "But there are sandwiches and yogurt. Make sure to have some fruit."

"Is cake a fruit?"

"It is not."

"Just checking."

I grabbed a turkey sandwich, some pineapple yogurt, and exactly twenty-three red grapes (I counted them, discarding a twenty-fourth grape because it failed the squishiness test) and sat in my room at my computer. Curious about Nate, I looked up "talking dog" and "mechanical dog nose" and "wind currents" and "largest horse of all time," the last of which had nothing to do with Nate, but, duh . . . monster horses are fascinating. There wasn't anything interesting on the first two searches, and the results on wind currents were far too technical, but the largest horse of all time was Sampson, a horse that could have won a battle with a dump truck.

"Mrrww?" I heard. I looked down. Snarls the cat had wandered into my bedroom. Snarls is Mom's cat. We are not friends. There have been *incidents*. Claws were involved. A birthday cake was destroyed.

"No," I said. Snarls only wanted to be friends with my sandwich, not me. I pushed him away with my toe and clicked my computer to the Pterodactyl Nest, the blog about Polt Middle that's named after our team mascot. We're the Crimson Pterodactyls.

It was time to do a little online reconnaissance.

First, I did a search for all my friends. Liz. And Stine. Ventura. A few others. There were all sorts of matches. Numerous articles. Various pictures. My hair looked weird in a lot of them.

Then I did a search for Nate. There were only a few matches, and most of them just had him tagged in the background of other people's photos, like when we were on a class field trip to the Schomburg Art Museum, and Kip Luppert was posing dramatically in front of a statue of a bear, and Nate was in the background staring at a painting of Albert Einstein.

"Hmm," I said, eating my sandwich and looking at the screen. None of my friends knew Nate. *Nobody* really knew Nate. Everyone thought he was sort of . . . boring.

"Hmm," I said, eating my twenty-third grape.

The next day, Liz Morris and I were sitting in the lush green courtyard in front of the Piltdown Mall, where we saw a man carrying the distinctive pink box of the Abracadabra Cake Shoppe, which is known to have the finest cakes in all of Polt. Cake makes me basically turn into a monster, much like a werewolf when it catches sight of the moon.

What I mean is I really like cake.

The man with the cake was wearing a black suit with red trim, and was possibly in his fifties. He had sunken cheeks, a gaunt appearance, a teacup in one hand, gray hair, heavy eyebrows, and the cake.

That man had cake.

This was a problem. I like cake, and it was Saturday, and on Saturday I am *supposed* to have cake. This is the *rule*. Saturday is the day of my weekly Cake vs. Pie club meetings, where my friends and I sit down and discuss the infinite merits of cake, and the admittedly delicious but much lesser merits of pie. And, at each meeting, some of us eat cake. The more foolish choose pie.

But the meeting had been canceled. Wendy Kamoss was at a family reunion. Buenaventura León, who we all call Ventura, was helping her mom with a garage sale. Stine—Christine Keykendall—had gone with her mom to choose a new bike, promising to keep my suggestion of "something with rockets" in mind. With Wendy, Ventura, *and* Stine out of the picture, that only left me and Liz Morris, meaning it would be far too dangerous to hold the meeting.

Liz is my best friend, but she is absolutely the enemy when it comes to cake versus pie, and Mom got mad the last time Liz and I debated one-on-one, even though the table was fine once we put it back into place and Liz's glasses didn't break when I knocked them off with the pillow and the bite mark on my shoulder cleared up after only a couple of days.

Liz ignored the man with the cake.

"So you were hanging out with Nate in the park? With *Nate*?" she asked.

I'd told Liz about meeting Nate. About the balloon. About Bosper. Well, at least I'd told her *parts* of what had happened, keeping the weirder parts to myself, meaning I'd barely told her anything.

Although, apparently even *that* had been too much. Liz was suspicious. I tried to give her a blank look.

"Hmm. Might there have been something more?" Liz said. "I can sense there's something you're not telling me. I have special *best-friend* powers, you know."

It was true. Liz and I could often read each other's minds, the way twins are supposedly able to do, even though we are not twins. She has short brown hair, while I have long red hair. My eyes are green. Hers are almost purple. Her ears stick out, but it's adorable. I have freckles, but they're equally adorable. I have a superhero lunch box, while Liz has one of a unicorn fighting Bigfoot. She's four feet nine inches, two inches taller than me. She is good with chopsticks, while I am not, as I'm sure the other regular customers at the Black Phantom Noodle Emporium will testify. Most telling of all, Liz prefers pie, while I prefer cake.

There is no way we are twins.

"No comment?" Liz said. "You're giving me the silent treatment?"

It had been less than a single second since she'd asked me about Nate, but Liz is impatient when it comes to secrets.

I said, "Nate is just—"

"Too late!" Liz interrupted, grabbing my phone. "Let's see if you two have been texting!"

"Gahh!" I said. "Liz!" I shrieked this loud enough that the man with the cake, disappearing into the distance, paused and looked back, so you would think that it would have been loud enough for Liz to hear it, since she was sitting right next to me. But, it was like she didn't even hear my first howl of protest, or the second one, or the third one, which I have to point out was one of my all-time best.

"Whoa," Liz said, looking at my phone, raising one eyebrow. "He *is* texting you."

It was true. There were two texts from Nate. The first was entirely blank, and the second one said, Sorry. That was from Bosper.

"Nate's dog sent you a text?" Liz asked.

"Nate's just joking," I said.

"He never seems like much of a joker in class," Liz said.

It's true that Nate usually keeps to himself in school. I used to think he was shy, or that he didn't have anything to say, but now I knew better. All those times I'd thought he was just being quiet, it's because he was almost certainly devising incredible inventions or solving unfathomable equations. He was being secretly . . . smart.

It was interesting to know he had secrets. But it was strange that I needed to have them now, too. From Liz.

During our walk home, I stole Liz's phone and looked up all the people she'd been texting.

This was entirely fair.

She'd done the same to me.

Unfortunately, there were no juicy secrets to be discovered on her phone. This meant that I was the only one with secrets, and that the man at the mall had been the only one with cake.

This was entirely unfair.

The walk home was nice, though. It only took us about a half hour. Polt isn't a very large city. But it's beautiful, with the hills, the trees, the river, and all the people who wave back when Liz dares me to wave at them. The weather tends to drizzle here, of course, so that Ventura says it's like the whole valley has the sniffles.

Luckily, it wasn't raining, so there were lots of people out, and we saw some cool robot paintings in a gallery window, and we saw police horses, and . . .

Nate.

He was walking along, wearing red goggles, with Bosper at his side, moving through the crowds on Gollow Avenue. It's the blocked-off street that's been turned into a pedestrian mall, where all the street performers play their banjos, or ride around on bicycles while wearing gorilla suits, or do circus gymnastics, or stand so still that it's like they're statues. Liz and I once earned twenty-four dollars making drawings of people for one dollar each. We'd given all the money to a woman with a trained turtle. It could sit on command, and it could . . . well, that's all it could do, but I like turtles and wanted to encourage further performances.

Weirdly, everyone seemed to be ignoring Nate, even though he had a measuring tape and was walking right up to people, measuring them and making notations in a little notebook. It was like he was invisible. I watched Nate walk up to a man in a checkered coat, measure the length of his coat, the length of his legs, and even the length of the burrito the man had just bought at a food cart. There was a woman in a blue sweater talking on a cell phone, laughing, expertly putting her hair into a ponytail with one hand. Nate held his measuring tape to the base of a nearby tree, and then Bosper—with the end of the measuring tape clamped in his mouth—padded over to the woman's legs and measured the distance. Nate seemed to think it was meaningful. He jotted something in his notebook, wrote something on his pants, and then began measuring the width of the bricks in the sidewalk.

Bosper saw me and yelled out, "Hello, the Delphine girl! Bosper is not talking in public because the dog is not supposed to!"

He was very proud of doing as he was told. Nate looked up and saw me, and he took off the strange red goggles and started to say something, but then he looked at Liz and paused, and he and Bosper turned around and walked off quickly in the other direction.

Weird.

"Wasn't that Nate?" Liz asked.

"Yes."

"Hmm," she said.

"What?"

"Usually you babble. But you only said 'Yes.' Just that one word."

"I don't usually babble. I just generally have stuff to say."

"A lot of stuff," Liz said.

"Piffle," I said.

I looked off down the block.

Through all the people.

To where Nate was receding into the distance.

I wondered when I would see him again.

chapter
2

Two hours later, I received an invite from Nate.

Liz had gone home and I was running an errand for my brother, Steve. He wanted to buy flowers for his latest girlfriend but didn't know which ones to buy, so he gave me seventeen dollars and thirty-five cents and threatened to tell Mom about the shaving cream thing if I didn't help him out. I had no choice but to go to Pioneer Square, where my favorite flower seller was working. Her name is Judi and the first time I ever saw her she was wearing a T-shirt with a drawing of an apricot and the words, "This is an apricot." I decided that I wanted to be her, or at least have her shirt, whichever was easier.

Judi is the set designer for all the plays at Polt Middle, Polt High School, and even the Polt Paramount Theater. She's the one who designed all the fake rocks for our school's production of *Captain Crater-Maker*, painted the background scenes for *Bigfoot vs. the Math Problem*, and of course she supplied all the roses and sunflowers for the dramatic ending of *The Ninja Who Needed a Hug*.

Judi and I were debating Steve's flowers when I looked down to see a precisely folded and hand-labeled note at my feet. It was triangle-shaped and had "Delphine" written on it with the most elaborate letters I'd ever seen, full of flourishes and swooping lines.

"What's this?" I said, picking up the note.

"Garbage," Judi said. "Trash can over here." She nudged a trash can with her boot.

"It has my name on it," I said.

"Really? There aren't many girls named Delphine. Even fewer boys. The note must be for you."

"Did you put it here?" This was exactly the sort of thing Judi would do. She's quirky. One time she came to work with all her clothes inside out, just to see if anybody would say anything. I did. I was the only one.

"Not me. Sure you didn't drop it?"

"I never had it."

Judi said, "Stop me if this is crazy, but maybe you could . . . *read* it?" She was snipping stems off the flowers. She does this so fast that I make sure to keep my fingers away from her. I don't want there to be any confusion.

I unfolded the note. A quarter fell out.

"The note came with a quarter," I said.

"Why is there a quarter?" Judi asked. We both thought about it. We both came up with nothing. Judi tapped on the note and said, "Read it."

I did.

It said:

*Delphine, this is Nate. Nate Bannister. The one with Bosper? Remember? The dog that grabbed the balloon? In the park? I put on that mechanical nose? Remember? We're going to be friends, so I hope you remember.*

I mumbled, "Yes. Hello? Of course I remember! Talking dogs. Mechanical noses. How could I *forget* something like that?"

The note said:

*I'm writing to invite you to my house. To my room. Is this socially awkward? I'm no good at being social. Here's my address. 417 NE 38th. It's the*

*corner of 38th and Pouch. It's pronounced "pooch."
Like a dog. I have a talking dog. Remember?*

"Your friend has a talking dog?" Judi asked. I'd forgotten I was reading out loud. This was not good.

"No," I said. It was perhaps the most brilliant cover-up in the history of espionage.

"He's inviting you to his room?" Judi asked. She was braiding several flowers into a wreath.

"He's not like that," I said.

"Sure."

"He's just . . . socially awkward."

"That's a boy for ya," Judi said. She was smiling in a way that meant she thought Nate was being a typical boy, but I knew he wasn't. He was being Nate. Entirely different.

"What's that?" Judi asked. She was pointing to the back of the note, where there was another message—one I'd lost in all the folds.

It said:

*Oh. Also, according to her blog, your brother's girlfriend likes peonies and snapdragons, so try to work some of them into a bouquet!*

*How did he know about the flowers?* I wondered as I walked from Judi's flower cart to the bus stop. I looked at the bouquet of peonies and snapdragons. *How did he know where to put the note?* The number 32 bus pulled up in front of me, and that's when I noticed something.

There was a note taped to the side of the bus shelter. It had my name on it.

*Delphine.*

The note said:

I'm not watching you or anything. I just have a formula for where you're most likely to be at any given point, what direction you'll be looking, and so on. I have similar charts for almost everyone.

I stepped up into the bus and put two dollars in the fare slot. The bus driver frowned at me.

"The fare is two dollars and twenty-five cents now," she told me. Her hefty shoulders shrugged. "Changed a couple of weeks back."

"Piffle," I said. I'd completely forgotten. "I only have two dollars. Could you please just . . . ?" I stopped because she was shaking her head.

"I'm really sorry, but management has been cracking down on—"

**28**

"Wait! I do have another quarter!" I reached into my pocket and produced the quarter I'd found in Nate's first note. Relieved, I slid it into the fare-taking machine-thingy, then found an empty seat.

I sat down.

Adjusted my backpack.

And then I saw a note taped to the side of the bus, just beneath the window.

It said "Delphine" on it.

I opened it up.

It said:

I calculated a strong possibility that you would forget the fare increase. This is because you're out of cereal and it's cloudy. Dead giveaway.

There were three more notes on my way home from school. One was on the bench at Plove Park, where I always get off the bus because I like to sit and look at the lake. Another was on the sidewalk half a block from my house, and the last was strapped to the Bakers' dog, Smoochy, who always runs out to see me. Together, the notes explained that Nate was having a serious problem and needed a friend to watch his back. He also wondered if I'd ever made out a will. The second note added that he was only joking about making out a will, and that the problem wasn't as dangerous as he'd made it sound. The third note apologized for being so vague in the first notes, and stated that the probability of my meeting an unfortunate end while helping him with the problem was no more than thirteen percent.

Thirteen percent.

chapter
3

Maybe it was reckless, but there are only so many chances in life to become friends with a talking dog. So I found myself walking to Nate's place, amazed by what had happened so far and wondering what would happen next. Because clearly, anything was possible and, let's face it, you can't suddenly find yourself in a world with talking dogs without wondering what *other* oddities are out there.

It was exciting.

It really was.

Some people don't like firsts. But for me, it's like an amusement park ride. You're twisting and turning and suddenly finding the bottom pulled out from under you, and all the time you're grinning and wondering, "What's next? What's *next*?" That's how I felt walking to Nate's house. I was whistling. I don't whistle very well, but I am enthusiastic, and that should count for something.

Nate met me at the door holding what looked like a crossbow that shot croquet balls, and a steaming cup of hot chocolate. He was looking everywhere, as if he was afraid I'd been followed. Bosper was on the roof, barking.

The house was two stories tall. There were quite a few trees. One of them, rising up from the backyard to loom in giant-like fashion over the house, had a tree-house with several different rooms. The treehouse had picture windows and a multitude of antennae. A model train track circumnavigated the treehouse's exterior.

"Were you attacked?" Nate asked. It was clear he believed this was a perfectly normal question.

"That's not a perfectly normal question," I said.

"Hold on. I need to shoot a ball of catnip." He strode across the front yard, aimed his crossbow at the street, and pulled the trigger. There was a *shoomp*-ing noise, and a grassy ball shot off from the crossbow to splatter all over the street.

"And *that* was most definitely not a normal thing to do," I told Nate.

"Hot chocolate is normal, though, right? I've warmed it to exactly one hundred and sixty-two degrees Fahrenheit, which I believe is the optimal temperature for warm beverages." He was handing me the hot chocolate, practically forcing me to take it.

"How did you know where to put all the notes?" I asked. The hot chocolate smelled fantastic. Steam was wafting up from the cup.

Nate was walking backward across his lawn, beckoning me to follow, keeping a watchful gaze for . . . *what*? I didn't know. But there was fully a thirteen percent chance of it being horrible.

"I didn't *exactly* know where to put the notes," he said. "I just calculated the highest probabilities. I left the same notes in several areas. Whichever ones you don't find are either collected by Bosper or Sir William."

"Sir William?" We'd almost reached his house, but Nate stopped and pointed to the sky. There was a gull flying around.

"That's him," Nate said. "The robot gull."

"Robot?" I peered closer.

Then it happened.

Out on the street, there was a screeching sound. Scraping metal. A muddy Ford truck shook, then tipped onto its side.

"Get in the house!" Nate yelled, grabbing my arm and tugging me in through the door, nearly spilling my hot chocolate. The door closed behind us with a vacuum

seal–like sound and Nate entered a code (I swear there were, like, sixty digits) and the entire house shivered.

"Safe!" Nate said. "Let's get lemonade! I get to be a host! I've never . . . I've never had a friend in my house before! This is exciting! Everyone else thinks I'm too strange to be friends with. Hold on to this crossbow, will you?" He handed me the crossbow and disappeared into the kitchen, leaving me behind as I wondered how in the world anybody could think Nate was strange. Nope. He was perfectly normal. Nothing to worry about. Cars suddenly flip over for no reason at all. Most of my friends have crossbows. The world is simply full of robot gulls.

The house shivered again and the door bulged inward. I shrieked and nearly fired a shot from the crossbow.

I ran into the kitchen to find Nate.

"Here's some lemonade," Nate said. "I put out some cookies. That was a good move, right? They're chocolate chip cookies. I have some ice cream, too. It's also chocolate chip. Oh. That wasn't smart, was it? I was trying for a chocolate chip theme, but I only had two items of chocolate chip nature, so that's not really a theme, more a lack of variety."

The floor trembled. Something huge had tumbled against the house. Outside, through the kitchen window, I could see Bosper leaping off the roof. He barked the whole way to the ground, then landed nimbly on his feet. He continued barking. I could not see what he was barking at. Honestly, there didn't seem to be anything to see. Then a tree broke off. The trunk just . . . snapped in half.

I said, "Nate? What's . . . ?"

"There are sun-ripened chips on the table. Better for you than regular potato chips. I put out some tortillas with hummus. Also jam. Jam and hummus. I know it's weird. Do you like olives?"

"Could we cool it with the snacks?"

He went pale. "You don't like them? Should I have made pasta? Yogurt? Girls love yogurt, right? All the television commercials make it seem like girls are very fond of yogurt. I could go to the store and get some, or send Sir William and—"

I grabbed Nate by the front of his shirt and pulled him very close, looking into his eyes. I think I may have even growled.

"Nate!" I roared. "What's attacking the house?" As if in response, the house shivered again. Something outside made a dreadful howl. It sounded like a very angry hurricane.

"It's a cat," Nate said.

"No. It's not." For a boy as smart as Nate, how could he be so ignorant about cats? Cats sleep. Cats chase after laser lights. Cats *ignore* you. Cats bask in windows. Cats purr and they eat and have I mentioned that they *sleep*? This is all very basic. At no point do cats tip over trucks or knock down trees. That is not a cat thing.

"It is," Nate said. "It's a cat. Can you, umm, let me go?"

"Oh, sorry," I said, releasing my grip.

He stepped back and bumped against the refrige-rator, which had several blueprints stuck in place with magnets, as well as multiple images of teacups with weird calculations written all over them. Nate's impact knocked one of the papers loose and it floated to the floor, wafting back and forth. On it was a strange symbol that looked like a family crest, with the entire world floating in a cup, and the words *Orbis Terrarum In A Vas*, which seemed to be in Latin, a language in which my proficiency is roughly equal to zero, give or take. Nate picked up the paper and put it back on the refrigerator, but then we both stumbled when the whole house shook, and the paper was once more jarred from the fridge to fall to the floor.

I picked it up.

Nate grabbed it from my hands so fast that it felt like I wasn't supposed to touch it, for some reason.

Putting it back on the fridge, he said, "Hey, Delphine, I was wondering, are there any big game hunters in your family? Any relatives who've gone on expeditions? Safaris? Stalking deadly beasts? That sort of thing? I could use someone with experience. Do you like bean dip?"

Bean dip and safaris? He was losing me again. I opened my mouth to speak, but at that moment something landed atop the house with a huge thud. The ceiling groaned in support of the strange new weight. I could hear the entire house creaking, straining.

"That's not a cat," I said, looking up.

"It's Proton," Nate said. "My mom's pet cat. I made him bigger."

"You made him bigger," I said. The house creaked again. "Of course you did. How big?"

"Not quite as big as an elephant."

"That was irresponsible," I said. For the life of me, I didn't know what else to say or do, so I sat down and began eating the chips and bean dip. They were really good. I mean, *seriously* really good.

"Are your parents home?" I asked. I was hoping they were, and that they had more experience than me with fighting giant cats. It wouldn't take much.

"Dad's off on a rock climb today," Nate said. "Won't be home until early Monday morning. Mom went with him. She wants to look for flowers she can plant in the garden."

"Flowers are nice," I said. The whole house shook again, as if it was disagreeing with me.

I ate more chips.

"I made those," Nate said, pointing to the chips. I realized I was only eating because I was nervous. A bad habit, I suppose, but it was exceptionally difficult to quit being nervous when a monster wouldn't quit attacking the house.

"You made them?" I asked.

"Engineered them, really. Nudged them toward more flavor."

"Nnak. Cow smarg rr u?" I was still eating the chips and bean dip, but I meant to say, "Nate. How smart are you?"

"Oh. Basically, umm, I suppose, in proportion to everyone else, I'm . . . How are the chips?" He reddened. I could see that he didn't want to talk about it.

"Wait," I said, a thought occurring to me. "If you're that smart—and you're *clearly* that smart—then how did this giant cat escape? Shouldn't you have taken precautions?" I could still hear the cat walking around on the roof. I was glad that Bosper wasn't up there anymore. I could hear him in the yard, growling and barking and yelling, "Cat!" He was barking so furiously that I don't think anyone could have understood him. At least, not any better than they could have understood me with a mouthful of chips and bean dip.

"Well, it was a Friday," Nate said.

"Okay." That meant nothing. Was he dumber on Fridays?

"Yesterday. Friday. The thirteenth."

"Okay." He still wasn't making sense. I knew the superstition thing of Friday the thirteenth, but even though a giant cat was screeching on the roof while a dog was talking in the yard, I wasn't about to believe in anything as weird as superstitions.

Nate said, "Well, I get bored."

"Okay," I said, and because he wasn't doing very well with his explanation, I added, "go on."

"So every Friday the thirteenth I schedule myself to do three, well, not-so-smart things."

"You schedule yourself to do three dumb things? That's not very smart at all!"

"I know!" he enthusiastically agreed. "But it doesn't count as one of the three things. I thought maybe it should for a while, but then I thought it defeated the purpose."

"But the reason to be so smart is to avoid doing stupid things!"

"No. It's to make life better. And sometimes a bit of chaos makes life better. Otherwise, everything is too predictable!"

"So . . . you do three dumb things?" I pushed the bowl of chips and bean dip away from me. I didn't want to eat them anymore. They might have been . . . dumb.

"Yesterday, I enlarged Proton. And I taught math to a caterpillar. And I sent a love letter to . . ." He faltered.

"You sent a love letter?"

"No." He waved his hands in a frantic "let's not talk about this" manner.

"Yes, you did. To who?"

"A . . . girl I met." He grabbed a cookie from the table and started chewing on it. He wasn't eating it. He was only chewing on it. I was about to ask him if he'd sent a letter to me (I hadn't gotten one, but it could still be in the mail) when a horrible noise came from the roof. It sounded like a giant cat was trying to dig through the roof of a house. It sounded *exactly* like that.

"He's trying to get in," Nate said. He frowned. "I didn't want to have to do this."

"Do what?" I was, at that moment, rather glad that it was Saturday the fourteenth. Whatever Nate was about to do, he was a day late for it to be idiotic.

"This." He opened a cabinet, but instead of glasses or plates or cereal boxes, there was an amazing array of computerized equipment. And buttons. Oodles of buttons. Twisty knobs. Electrical arcs. Keypads. It looked like a NASA control room.

I said, "Nathan Bannister. Explain." I pointed to the cabinet so he would know *exactly* what I wanted him to explain. I had to yell in order to be heard over the roar of the cat digging on the roof. The whole house was trembling. Bosper, outside, was scrambling up onto the windowsill, trying to get to the roof. I wasn't sure what he would do up there. The terrier was capable of speech, but I doubted he was capable of challenging a creature several hundred times his size. Dogs will be dogs, I guess.

Nate said, "This is my command center for the house. Well, one of them, anyway." He pulled out a drawer so that he could use it as a step, crawling up onto the counter to reach the cabinet better.

"Command center?"

"All the defenses. And the weapons."

I said, "You've weaponized your house?" This came out as more of a squeak than a question.

"Oh, yeah," Nate said. He was twisting at knobs, entering commands on a keyboard, and, for some reason, drawing a smiley face on a touch pad. "But only a little. And nothing dangerous. Only a few scent-blasters to drive away certain animals. Then there's a force field, but I ran out of AAA batteries. And I have a nuclear whistle for driving off dogs, from the smallest mutt to, well, even a nuclear Rottweiler, if one of those happens to attack. I also have a few atomic squirt guns, an electric field discharger, a mechanical ghost for scaring away superstitious people, and a giant laser."

"You have a giant laser? I thought you said there was nothing dangerous! I've seen lasers in movies! They're mainly used for blasting spaceships into very tiny pieces! They're dangerous!" I used the open drawer to crawl up onto the counter next to Nate, poking him in the arm. He winced.

"It's not really a laser," he said. "It's a laser pointer. A huge one. I've been trying to design a way to project video-game holograms into the sky. Haven't quite worked it out yet, but it should be able to keep Proton occupied long enough for us to find the six messages."

"The six messages? What six messages? Do you know that you have an infuriating way of not telling me what's happening?" He nodded and smiled in a way that said, *yes*, he did indeed know all about that, but he wasn't going to do much about it.

"I'll tell you about the six messages in a bit. Here. Put these on. You'll be able to see better." From another kitchen cabinet, Nate had grabbed three pairs of goggles. They looked almost like swimming goggles, except with red lenses and something like a cell phone attached to the straps.

I put on the goggles. Nothing changed.

"These don't work," I said. I'm going to go right ahead and be honest here and admit that I was actually happy they didn't work. It made me feel like I'd gotten one up on Nate.

"Wait for it," he said. "They'll work soon enough." Then he took my hand and led me toward the front door.

"We're going *out* there?" I said. The tone in my voice

made it clear that I was not in favor of this. It's not that I don't like cats; I just don't like cats that are almost nearly the size of an elephant. That's a big difference. Literally.

"We have to go out if we're going to find the six messages," he said. "Besides, Bosper will protect us."

"No, he won't! He's too small! Unless . . . Nate, you're not going to make *him* big, too, are you?"

Nate said, "Don't be ridiculous. Why would I make a giant dog?" I kept my mouth shut, but of course the obvious question was, *Why would you make a giant cat?*

The door opened.

Nate pulled me outside.

Bosper came running up to us and said, "Big cat! I've been barking! What a good boy!" Nate petted his head and put the third pair of goggles over the terrier's eyes.

"These don't work!" Bosper said.

I said, "Hah!"

"Wait for it!" Nate said. He sounded exasperated, but since he was the cause of all the problems, I thought it was somewhat rude for him to—

A giant cat looked down over the edge of the roof. I made a noise. It was close to a scream, just much louder.

"There!" Nate said, gesturing to a colossal feline who seemed quite ready to pounce on us. "I've calibrated the goggles to see invisible cats. Of course you wouldn't have seen anything inside the house. But there, now, look! See!"

"Piffle!" I said. And then, "RUN!"

"Brilliant!" Nate said.

We ran.

It was no good trying to outrun Proton, of course. No good at all. The cat leaped from the roof and landed on the street with a noise like an entire football game condensed into a single sound. The ground shook. Bosper resumed barking.

Nate said, "We'll be okay! Proton won't leave the yard."

"He's already in the street!" I said. Well, *screamed*.

"True enough. Okay. But he'll have to go back to the yard in a bit because of the sonic leash. I turned it on when we were in the kitchen."

"Of course," I said, as if I'd been studying sonic leashes just that very morning and knew all about them.

"It has to do with quarks," Nate said. He was trying to be helpful because he'd seen the confusion in my eyes, though he'd apparently missed the terror.

"And a singularity point of oscillations," Nate added, helpfully. He made a series of gestures with his hands. I believe he was trying to indicate a singularity point of oscillations. I made gestures with my hands as well. I was trying to signify that Nate should shut up, and that we should run.

The giant cat was coming closer, stalking us. His eyes were each the size of my entire head, and his whiskers were the length of my arm span. He was making a growl that I could feel in my chest, the way I feel when I'm at a concert and stand too close to the speakers, or the way it feels when I stand next to the ocean and there's all this overwhelming power that's roaring and rumbling. His claws were as long as kitchen knives. His teeth were even longer. He had orange and white fur, with a concentration of orange around his eyes, shaped like the Lone Ranger's mask. It would have looked funny when he was normal size, but he was not normal size and it was not funny and I was not having fun. The ground did a bass-drum thump when Proton leaped into the air, pouncing, and coming right for—

"Look out!" I yelled, and I knocked Nate aside, saving him from the cat. It was ridiculously noble of me.

Also, unnecessary.

The giant cat swerved in midair.

He *swerved*.

Proton tumbled end over end and did not land on his feet. He landed on a birdbath, crushing it. Bosper was barking at him.

"Let's run!" Nate said, taking my hand again. We ran out into the street, heading in the direction of a car parked along the curb, maybe a half block down. It was colored green and had a painting of Einstein on the driver's door. Also, the license plate was WAIT4IT. It was obviously Nate's family car. Were we going to hide there? Was there something important inside?

"What just happened?" I asked, looking back to the yard.

"Bosper got him with the sonic leash. Wow. You sure ask a lot of questions."

"I'm finding a lot of things questionable," I said. "What do you mean, your terrier got him with a sonic leash?"

"The leash is somewhat like a whip. Or, I guess, a force field. It's too complex to go into right now. And, I didn't mean it was bad that you're asking questions. I think it's great. People should always ask questions. Asking questions is like bodybuilding for the brain. Here, get in the car."

"Who's going to drive?" I asked.

"I will."

"You?" Yet another question. My brain was going to be super-buff.

"Do you seriously think someone with my IQ can't drive a car? And, the windows will project holograms, so I'll look like a middle-aged balding guy to anyone who looks at the car."

"What will I look like?"

"A pretty girl," he said. He shifted the car to drive, and we went roaring off down the street. Nate had his seat all the way forward and was sitting on a stack of laptop computers.

"You made a hologram of a pretty girl?" I asked. Everything I said was a question.

"No," Nate said. "There's no hologram for you. You'll just appear as you normally do."

"Oh," I said. "Oh. Oh, okay." I sat back in my seat. I felt a bit tingly. Some of it was having been attacked by a giant cat, but another part of it was Nate's answer. That's just the truth.

No question.

# chapter 4

After a frantic car ride to the center of downtown, Nate hustled me down the busy sidewalk next to all the expensive clothing stores. We were in a rush. People shopping in the fancy stores gave us odd looks. Maybe they could sense that we were two adventurers on an important quest. Or, possibly they thought our red goggles were strange. It was a fair guess.

"We need to find the six messages," Nate explained. "When combined, they contain the formula that will return Proton to his normal size. They're out *there*." He pointed expansively in front of us.

"Why don't we already have this formula?" I asked. "Don't you know it?"

"I did, but I intentionally forgot."

"Why would you do such a thing?"

"Because I like to be challenged. Far too many people lead dull lives, never stretching their boundaries, content to do the same things over and over again. Every day is strictly routine, as if life were an equation they've already solved, and they're satisfied with their grades and don't want to do anything except sit on their couches for the remainder of their lives."

"Without ever being attacked by a giant cat."

"Exactly!" Nate said, agreeing with me, as if he'd never heard of sarcasm before.

"So what *are* these six messages?" I asked.

"Parts of a formula that I gave to some of our classmates."

"You did? Which ones?"

"Vicky Ott. Kip Luppert. Marigold Tina. Ricky Zander's older brother. Susan Heller. Jaime Huffman's goldfish."

"You gave an important secret formula to a goldfish?"

"Yes, I did. Well, you have to understand that the messages are written on a series of conjoined molecules. It's not like I stuffed a sheet of paper into a goldfish bowl. I'm not crazy."

I discreetly coughed.

Nate said, "The actual messages are smaller than the eye can see. Nobody even knows they're carrying them. All I have to do is scan the molecules, assemble

**50**

the results, make the serum, give it to Proton, and then it's all over."

"I like how you're talking about forcing giant cats to take serums as if it was no big deal."

"And I like that you're not freaking out. I've never had a friend that wasn't, well, too scared to be my friend." He gave me a quick hug. I sighed.

"Who's first?" I asked. "I just can't wait to scan molecules." It was probably the first time I'd ever spoken that particular sentence.

"Ricky Zander's older brother works as a model right up here, at Pottlebarn Fashions, and he's scheduled to work today."

"He works as a model? Really?"

"Sure. Didn't you know that? I can't be the only one who keeps a complete dossier on all my classmates, can I?"

"Nate, I'd say you're very probably the only one who keeps a complete dossier on all their classmates, yes."

"Weird."

"Not weird."

We'd reached Pottlebarn Fashions. It was decidedly fashions for the rich. The window to the right of the door displayed mannequins in very nice suits. Very *expensive* suits. The price tags were all in the thousands of dollars. Do people really pay that much for a suit? For anything?

I suppose they must. I'm hardly an expert on fashion, as my mother is all too willing to point out. I prefer sneakers. Capri pants. Simple shirts. Sometimes a skirt. My friend Liz says I look like a fashion model on her day off.

We went inside the store, where Nate handed me his phone, smiling. "Check this out," he said. It had a live video feed of Proton chasing after the huge laser pointer dot in Nate's yard. The giant cat was leaping everywhere, tearing up the yard. Bosper was barking and barking. I took off my goggles and looked again. It was only the laser dot. And poor Bosper. I put my goggles back on. The cat was back.

"Can I help you?" a clerk said. I jumped and hid Nate's phone behind my back. Then I felt silly. He couldn't even see the cat, anyway.

"I'm looking for a birthday present," Nate said. The clerk smiled at us. It was the smile that adults give me when they think I'm acting childish. The clerk (who looked like a bearded scarecrow in a very nice suit) patted Nate on the shoulder.

"You should try a toy store, kid. What do you want for your birthday? A rocket ship?"

Nate said, "If I wanted a rocket ship, I'd build one. Do you know what this is?" Nate reached into his back pocket and produced a credit card. It had a symbol I'd never seen before. The card was transparent, and the symbol was a stylized elephant's head in gold. The card had Nate's name, a series of numbers, and the letter *a*, in large size.

"Oh," the clerk said. His face went white. He stumbled a bit and grabbed on to a counter for support. "Is that . . . is that . . . ?"

"A gold elephant card?" Nate said. "Yes. It is. You've heard of them, then?"

"The Legendary Credit Card," the clerk said. He didn't just say "legendary credit card." He said *Legendary Credit Card.* I could hear the capital letters.

"What's a gold elephant card?" I

asked Nate, but he didn't get a chance to answer.

"What can I do for you, sir?" the clerk asked, entirely gushing, pushing me aside in his eagerness to talk with Nate.

Nate said, "Something in gabardine. A classic look. Six-on-two double-breasted." I was as lost as when he was talking about quarks and black holes.

Nate added, "And if you could bring out some models, that would be fantastic."

"Of course! Of course!" the clerk said, clapping his hands nervously. "And, if I might say so, sir, the goggles you and your young lady are wearing are quite fetching. Absolute top-notch!"

"They help us see invisible cats," Nate said.

"Quite nice," the clerk said, entirely unfazed. "Shall we head into the viewing room?"

We did head into the viewing room, where we sat on a couch that was as soft as a rabbit's belly. A waiter (yes, a waiter in a clothes store!) brought us some bite-size cucumber sandwiches and then stared at us and stared at us until I wondered if we were supposed to tip him. Nate, however, seemed entirely at ease.

"Just water will do," he said. "Noncarbonated, if you will." At this, the waiter heaved a sigh of relief and went off, returning shortly with glasses of water served in tall cocktail glasses. Nate whispered to me, "It's customary to serve champagne during these viewings, but we're too young. The waiter didn't know what to do. Decorum and all that."

"Decorum and all that," I agreed.

Soon, one by one, a parade of suits strode past us, posing, and I have to tell you that the land of luxurious men's fashions is crackingly boring. The clerk would gleefully explain the wonders of each suit, talking about the fabric, the sewing, the craft, and so on and so forth, but I'd spent the morning being menaced by a giant cat, meaning that looking at suits was a pale and distant second in terms of excitement. I knew we were looking for Ricky's brother, but couldn't they hurry it up already?

One by one, Nate turned each suit down. He would say, "Hmm. No," and then the clerk would say, "Of course not!" and herd the model out while complimenting Nate's fine taste in fashion and apologizing for even presenting such an abomination as *that* suit, *this* suit, or the *other* suit.

Finally, Nate perked up when it was Ricky's brother's turn to pose. "Hmm, this suit," Nate said, interested for the first time.

"Ahh-hahh!" said the clerk.

Nate stood and walked around Ricky's brother, nodding, considering, and I had no idea at all what he was doing, but I was growing more comfortable with that, as I was beginning to understand that Nathan Bannister would always be a mystery to me.

"Yes," Nate finally said. "I think this will do. Three of them, then. One cut for evening. Another for yachting. A third for the casual day."

"Ahh, the good life," the clerk said. "And in a good suit."

"I'll have Father's measurements sent around," Nate said. He reached back into his pocket and produced that credit card again. The clerk went giddy.

"Shall I mention the cost?" the clerk asked, which I thought was very strange. *Of course* you mention the cost! How would anyone know if they could afford something if they don't know what it costs?"

"Mention the cost?" Nate said, clearly insulted. Apparently, I was wrong.

"My apologies, sir!" the clerk said in hasty fashion. "Some people want to know." His voice went lower and in a conspiratorial tone he said, "*Other* people." Then he and Nate laughed heartily.

And Nate accidentally dropped his credit card.

The clerk gasped as if he was afraid it would shatter.

"I'll get that for you, sir," Ricky's brother said. While he bent down to retrieve the credit card, Nate took out a strange and curious device from his pocket. It looked like a small slingshot, but instead of a rubber band it had arcs of electricity. Nate touched it to the back of Ricky's brother's neck. Nothing happened. Nothing that I could tell, at least. The model didn't even react. But Nate was clearly satisfied, tucking the bizarre slingshot back out of view. The model straightened, holding the credit card out to Nate. His hands were shivering.

"T-this is a gold elly-a-phant c-card," he said. He was having trouble speaking.

"Yes," Nate said, supremely unconcerned. He took

the card from the model and handed it to the clerk, who drooled a bit. His knees even trembled.

The clerk left through a curtained doorway. The model excused himself and departed. Nate and I were only alone for a few seconds, as two musicians entered the room and, without so much as a "Hello, how's your day?" they started playing. One had a strange-looking guitar and the other a violin. They played very softly, as if afraid they would frighten us.

Oblivious to the music, Nate scribbled some equations on his hand. I had no idea what he was doing or what would happen next. But Nate did. I'm not sure exactly *why* I was trusting a boy I'd just met, one who had created a giant rampaging cat and who'd given a secret message to a goldfish, but . . .

I felt good when he was around.

I asked Nate, "What's a gold elephant credit card?"

"Oh. Uhh. Nothing." His cheeks reddened from embarrassment.

"C'mon, spill. I'm a founding member of the Get Chased by a Giant Cat Club, so you're not allowed to keep secrets from me. What's a gold elephant card?"

"A rare credit card," Nate said. "Only really, uhh, that is, you have to . . . only rich people have them."

"How rich?"

"This music is nice, right?"

"How can you be as smart as you are and not know when you're beaten? How rich? Tell me."

"Really rich. Like, mega-rich."

"Colossally and cosmically super-rich?" I asked. Nate thought about it. Nodded.

"So, how many of these cards are there? Fifty thousand? Twenty thousand?"

"Three."

"Three thousand? Worldwide? That *is* rare."

"No. Three. Just three."

"Nate!" I said. I took a few breaths. "Are you telling me you're like . . . one of the three richest people in the world?" I was shrieking, because I couldn't believe it, but I was also hissing, because I didn't want the musicians to overhear us.

Nate was silent.

I poked him.

I said, "Nate. Seriously. You're one of the three richest people in the world?"

He said, "Well. Umm. I'm . . . one of them. Yes."

I just looked at him, trying to think of what to say, wondering how many other secrets Nathan Bannister was holding back. It was going to be . . . *interesting* getting to know him. And I suppose it didn't matter much that he'd avoided telling me he was one of the richest people on earth. We all have our secrets, and it's not like I was going to tell him about the songs I make up in the shower or the songs I make up in my bedroom or the songs that Liz and I sang on top of Polt Middle before we were very sternly warned not to sneak up there anymore, and only did it four more times afterward. So far.

"And, here we are, sir!" the clerk said, striding back into the room and reluctantly returning Nate's credit card. "Is there anything else I can help you with? Anything at all?"

"That will be all, for now," Nate said. We turned to go.

The clerk said, "A note of interest, sir. I've just had a chat with the manager, and we've decided to branch out into the field of goggles. Goggles with red lenses. We're ever so inspired by the ones you and your charming friend are wearing. We envision an entire product line!"

"How interesting," Nate said. "I think you can count on seeing me again."

The clerk beamed. He smiled. He let out a joyful sigh, and his fingers were trembling as he held the curtains aside so that Nate and I could leave.

"So, we found Ricky Zander's older brother," I said, once we were on the sidewalk. "That slingshot thing, what did that do?"

"Decoded the molecule. Here."

Nate showed me a readout on his phone. It was a long series of numbers and letters and a few symbols that looked like squiggles or ink blots. I was disappointed. Secret messages are supposed to be interesting and mysterious, like, "The raven burps when dogs eat macaroni," or "The caped man's smile is five snakes long." But, no, it was just a bunch of random characters.

"So, what now?" I asked.

"We locate Susan Heller next and retrieve her part of the formula. I sent her . . . never mind."

"You sent her something? What?"

"Nothing. A shoe catalog. I mean, an invitation to a party. No, I'm not having a party. I never have parties. You'll know I'm lying. I shouldn't have said that. I should think of something else. Something believable."

"Uh, Nate?" I reminded him. "Standing right here." He was obviously talking to himself. Fidgeting. Biting his lip and twirling his fingers. There was a single bead of sweat on his forehead, and there hadn't been any sweat at all when Proton the giant cat was chasing after us, even though the cat was nearly almost as big as an elephant. Nate took off his goggles, blinked, put them back on, and said, "Need to think. Need to think. Hmm. Not-math is hard. Oh! I've got it!" He turned to me and said, "I sent her some homework assignments. She has me look over them to make sure she's doing them correctly."

I just looked at him.

He looked at me. His fingers continued to twitch.

Finally, Nate said, "Oh. Was some of my internal dialogue . . . external?" There were red tinges at the sides of his face, as if a blush were in the starting block, ready to surge forward at a moment's notice.

"Yes. You were trying to think of something believable, which means . . . let's see, you're hiding something. So, she's the one you sent the love letter to, isn't she?" I crossed my arms in front of me, much like Mom stands when she's caught Dad doing something wrong.

"Susan and I are on . . . some . . . yearbook thing together?" Nate said. It was a lousy try.

I said, "Gosh, I hope *my* internal dialogue doesn't spill out. But, what if it does? Then Nate will know I'm thinking about clobbering him. And also that it's none of my business who he sends love letters to. Why would I care? All I care about is stopping a giant cat. Also, Nate is an idiot."

I paused meaningfully.

Nate said, "I don't think I've ever been called an idiot before!" He was beaming. He reached out, grabbed me, and gave me a hug.

"I feel great!" he said. He was positively glowing now.

"Um, Nate. Being called an idiot is bad."

"Oh, no no no," Nate said, waggling a finger at me. "It's fantastic. Because, if you're an idiot, that means you have a lot to learn!"

"Uh, okay."

"And learning is fun!"

"Uh, okay."

Nate looked at me, smiled, stared into my eyes, and said, "Delphine Cooper. You are an idiot!"

"What!" Now he was calling *me* a name? *Me*? I tried very hard to control my temper. I had to close my eyes. I had to repeat a few words in my head. *Good girls are not supposed to punch boys. Good girls are not supposed to punch boys. Good girls are hardly ever supposed to punch boys.*

"I meant that as a compliment," Nate said.

I said, "I can't hear you. My eyes are closed."

"That doesn't make sense, Delphine."

"Mom says girls don't need to make sense."

"Yeah," Nate said. "Dad says the same thing. A lot." I opened my eyes and peeked at what Nate was doing. He was holding some sort of device. It looked like a handheld computer game, but there were only streams of numbers on the display. I peeked my eyes open a bit more.

"Can you actually read that?" I asked. The numbers were going by so fast and they were just . . . numbers.

"Sure!" Nate said, as if anybody should be able to under-stand the quickly changing display. "They're numbers! But . . . something's wrong." He frowned.

"Wrong?"

"Susan *always* goes shopping on Saturdays, but something has changed. Some outside influence is intruding. I'd thought we could just find her at the mall, but she's at an airfield." He held up the device to show me. It did not have a picture of Susan Heller at an airfield. It also did not have a text message saying, "Susan Heller is at an airfield." It was just a string of numbers. I nodded as if they meant something to me.

Nate said, "This can't be a coincidence. The proba-bility of Susan shopping on Saturdays is in the upper ninety-ninth percentile." He showed me the device again. It was a huge sprawl of numbers running around, enthusiastically being numbers. I shook my head in a knowing fashion, rather than pointing out that my odds of understanding what he was showing me were in the lower first percentile.

"So," Nate said. "This means there's a near certainty that some outside force is trying to keep Susan away from us, just when we need her. Somebody is trying to stop us."

"Stop us?"

He showed me the numbers again. They were still numbers. They might well have been different numbers.

Who knows? There seemed to be a lot of nines. Was that significant?

"Lot of *nines*, there," I said.

"Good catch," Nate said. "It's very significant. It means someone is working against us. It means ... today just became more interesting."

I looked around at the people walking by on the sidewalk, all these strangers moving around us. I was thinking about murderous giant cats and how someone, somewhere out there, possibly someone very near, was apparently on the side of the *cat*, or at least not on *our* side.

Nate had said that was interesting.

I guess that's one definition.

After we left the Very Expensive Men's Fashion Store, we only walked about ten feet before Nate suddenly stopped. We were talking about dogs, and about how they were once wolves, tens of thousands of years ago, and about what they might be tens of thousands of years in the future. I was arguing that they would be robots, because everything will be robots in the future. Nate was just starting to debate my unshakeable premise, but then he stopped. Just ... stopped in the middle of the sidewalk. And he stopped with that gasp you see in horror movies. Because of this, I was expecting to see an assassin in a hockey mask, or a demon crawling up from the sewers, or something more interesting than what Nate was actually looking at.

There were three teacups on the sidewalk, up against the building. Somebody had left them there.

Apparently Nate was frightened of *litter.*

It is unsightly, and people really should clean up after themselves, but I couldn't understand why Nate looked so entirely unsettled.

He took a few calming breaths, and then he had his smile back.

We started walking again, and I forgot about the teacups. I didn't think they were any big thing.

But I would find out I was wrong in only ten more steps when we reached the car.

Nate took a deep breath and said, "Delphine, I've been thinking I should probably mention death. And tea. Death and tea."

I said, "What?" I put a lot of questions into that one simple word.

Nate had grown distracted after seeing the teacups, mumbling about statistics and shuffling along, tripping over his own feet, which wasn't like him at all.

Nate explained, "You probably know that tea is a drink made by combining hot water and tea leaves.

Death, as you also probably know, is what can happen when you fight giant cats, or when an international criminal organization decides you're too dangerous to their taking-over-the-world plans and resolves to have you eliminated. There are many other causes of death, but those are the two we should probably focus on for today."

That explained nothing. "What?" I said again, in a bit of a daze.

Nate went on. "Tea and death. But not just *any* tea and not just *any* death. I'm specifically talking about the Red Death Tea Society."

I repeated, "What?" I was on a roll.

Nate got into the car and opened my door. I got inside and immediately put on my seat belt.

He said, "Have you heard of them? Probably not, because the Red Death Tea Society is very secretive and has some rather foul methods of ensuring its agents never spill its secrets. I'll give you a hint of the penalty in such cases: they do not give tea to the traitors. They give them the other thing."

I said, "The other thing? So, not tea but—oh. I see." I checked my seat belt. It seemed important. Before I met Nate I'd never heard of such things as the Red Death Tea Society. Really, the direst organization that had ever entered my life was my Cake vs. Pie debating society, where I'm hardly ever thinking about murder. In fact, I'm not thinking about murder at all.

Nate said, "Maybe I'm just being paranoid, but this thing with Susan *not* going shopping on a Saturday is too much of a statistical anomaly. Someone is clearly interfering with the parameters of this experiment."

"And you think it's these Red Death guys?" I checked my seat belt. It was still on. Nate talking about being paranoid had made me paranoid.

Nate said, "It's one possibility. A very high possibility. And, well, you saw the teacups. The point is, the Red Death Tea Society *does* exist, and while their tea is, without question, excellent . . . they are even more excellent at doing the death thing. They've already asked me to join their ranks several times, but of course I've refused. I'm charting a high probability that they will soon try to . . . get rid of me."

"Get rid of you?" I said. "That sounds bad."

"Yes. It is."

"Is your seat belt on?" I asked.

"Yes," Nate said.

"Good."

"Agreed. It's definitely for the best, since, for all we know, Sir Jakob Maculte—the twenty-seventh lord of Mayberry Castle and the leader of the Red Death Tea Society—is right now writing my name on a piece of ancient parchment, sliding it inside a leather envelope, sealing it with a combination of wax, tea leaves, and a pinprick of his own blood, and then handing it to an assistant with orders to deliver it to an extremely talented group of assassins."

"That sounds dramatic."

"It's the way they work. Drama is basically their thing. And tea, of course."

"So, how many of these guys are out there? Ten? Twenty?"

"Ah. No. More like a few thousand. Men and women of all ages. Maculte, their leader, has a mind nearly the equal of mine."

"Nearly?"

"Technically speaking, he might be smarter than me, but his inventions aren't . . . inventive. He lacks spark, spirit, whimsy."

"Hmm," I said, thinking that Nate might sometimes be *too* whimsical. We were, after all, on the trail of a whimsically giant cat.

"And Luria Pevermore is second in command," Nate said. "This is her." He showed me a picture on his phone. She was maybe in her late twenties. Her hair was a darker red than mine, but while mine tends to curl, hers was silky and straight and down to her shoulders. She had green eyes, high cheekbones, a few freckles. She was wearing a dress and smiling at the camera with a wide mouth, although the smile was the opposite of friendly. Even though she was beautiful, she mostly looked like someone who enjoyed squishing flies.

"Luria is an incredible chemist," Nate said. "She's in charge of making all the teas the Red Death Tea Society drinks. She also makes other things."

"Other things?" I asked. Nate had made it sound ominous.

"Yes," Nate said. "Other things. And if that sounded ominous, it should have, because Luria makes such things as a potion that erases your memory, and one that turns your arms into charcoal-flavored pudding, and one that makes you disappear."

"An invisibility potion?" I asked. "That's kind of neat."

"I didn't mean invisibility," Nate said. His voice had gone even more super-ominous, though also a bit squeaky. "I meant you disappear. Entirely. Forever. You're just . . . gone."

"Piffle," I said. "I don't like Luria. What's this Maculte guy look like? You have him on your phone?"

"Yes," Nate said. "I took a picture of him once when he was trying to trigger a new ice age. It's a better photo than the one from when he was trying to change Polt's water supply into a mind-control serum, because the lightning flashes ruined that one. I wish the photo I took during the time Maculte was trying to replace my mom and dad with robots would have turned out better, but it was too dark in the volcano when—"

"How many times have you fought this guy?" I asked.

"Only three times," Nate said, bringing up the photo on his phone.

"Oh," I said. Three times? That wasn't quite as bad as I'd been fearing. Although of course three tries at destroying the world, or destroying Polt, or at least destroying Nate, that was three times too—

"Wait," Nate said, handing me his phone. "Did you mean how many times I've fought the Red Death Tea Society? Because *that* would be twenty-seven times. But I've only met Maculte three times, and that last time in that volcano he was wearing a full asbestos suit to protect him from the heat, so there wasn't much of a reason to take a photo, although the glow from the lava was dramatic and—"

"Arrkk!" I said. It was a scream.

"What's wrong?"

"Piffle," I said. It was a growl.

"Delphine?"

"*This* is Maculte?" I said, looking at the image on Nate's phone, which was of a man wearing a black suit with red trim, a man who was possibly in his fifties, a man with sunken cheeks, a gaunt appearance, a teacup in one hand, gray hair, and heavy eyebrows. He was not, however, carrying a cake, like he had been when I saw him outside the mall.

"Yes," Nate said. "That's Maculte. Why?"

"I saw him. At the mall." I was checking my seat belt again. I wanted more seat belts. I wanted *all* the seat belts.

"Oooo," Nate said. "He must be investigating you. Seeing if you're a threat."

"I don't really feel like a threat. I feel like going home and hiding under the bed. How long do you think he's been spying on me?"

"Hard to tell. The Red Death Tea Society has thousands of spies. It's always difficult to tell who might be working for them, other than how they all have a tattoo of a tea leaf on their . . . well, let's say their buttock regions."

"They tattoo tea leaves on their butts?"

"They do. Incidentally, have you seen anyone with a tea leaf tattooed on their butt?"

"I have not," I said. "But I haven't really been looking."

We drove along in silence for a while, heading toward wherever Nate had hidden the next of the six messages. I was wondering where that might be. I was wondering quite a few things, honestly. For instance, as the blocks of office buildings turned into the quaint homes of Polt suburbia, I looked at the people on the sidewalks, wondering if any of them was an assassin for a secret society intent on taking over the world. I glared at a few of them, just in case.

"Are you okay?" Nate asked, after a bit. "You're unusually quiet. I have charts of how often you speak, and you're in the upper ninety-eighth percentile for conversation."

"I'm fine. It's just a lot to take in."

"And you're angry, too."

"I am?" I hadn't known I was mad, but now that Nate mentioned it, I certainly was. The Red Death Tea Society sounded like a big bunch of bullies, and I don't like bullies. I suppose no one does.

"Statistically speaking, you're probably mad," Nate said. "That's because you have red hair. It's beautiful red hair, but, yes, that means you have an eager temper."

"Red-haired people get mad more often?"

"No. Not really. I was just joking with you, because I thought you might be getting nervous after finding out about a death cult."

I wasn't sure what to say here, so I adjusted my seat belt.

"Yes," he said. "It made me tense when I first found out, too. What helps me, though, is to think about how, somewhere out there in the world, there's a tattoo artist who spends his entire day doing nothing except tattooing tea leaves on the butt of every new agent." He looked over to me and smiled. I tried to smile back.

A block went by.

And another.

Finally, I said, "All day long. Tattoo after tattoo. Butt after butt. That's ridiculous."

"It is!" Nate said. And he started to laugh, and I started to laugh along with him.

But I kept my seat belt on.

It was a good thing I kept my seat belt on.

We'd only gone two blocks when Nate said, "Hmm." I didn't pay much attention to this at first, because Nate is pretty much always mumbling. Sometimes he's just saying numbers. But then, just a bit farther on, he said it again.

"Hmm," he said. He was looking out the window.

And then, "Hmm," he said. He was looking forward, down the street.

A half block farther, he rolled down his window, sniffed, and said, "Hmm."

And then, in the next block we drove past Lieber's Kite Store and I was thinking of telling Nate about how they can make kites with your picture on them, and how Liz Morris and I made kites of ourselves in fighting poses and then tried to have a kite fight, but the wind near Coover Lake was so strong that we were mostly just digging our kites out of the sand where they'd crashed. But before I could say anything, Nate's attention was suddenly riveted on the sidewalk, where I could see nothing of any particular notice except a couple of discarded cups that were blowing along in the breeze.

And Nate said, "Hmm."

That doesn't sound very dire, but it was the *way* he said it. It wasn't a "hmm" of "perhaps I shouldn't have eaten an extra burrito" but rather a "hmm" of "I'm suspecting something catastrophic is going to happen, such as an imminent attack by an unsavory organization of tea-drinking assassins." You'll have to take my word for it that there's a particular way of saying "hmm" that sounds just like that.

Still, nothing happened. We continued driving. All the while, Nate checked the side mirrors, the rearview mirror, and also some interesting digital readouts on the car's dashboard, which mostly looked like we were driving a time-traveling warp-drive-capable spaceship rather than a mostly-average-but-interestingly-painted car. There were so many readouts that they partially overlapped, and they all had numbers and some of them had pulsing dots and some of them were views of the car from various angles, seen from afar, like little movies of us driving down the street. I asked Nate about those and he explained that he was tapping into security cameras and satellites to film the surrounding area, to make sure we were safe.

"And, *are* we safe?" I asked.

"Hmm," he said.

"That's not really an answer," I said. "That's the sort of thing my dad says to my mom when he doesn't want to answer. Or, to be fair, when *Mom* doesn't want to answer something that Dad—"

"Hmm," Nate said, interrupting me, staring out his window. We were stopped at a red light, and Nate was looking out the window to the corner, obviously concerned. I didn't see anything to be concerned about. Just a newspaper dispenser and two people standing next to it, waiting for the light to change. One of them was a young woman wearing headphones, jogging in place. The other was an older man with a full beard, talking on a cell phone, having a drink from a Styrofoam cup.

"What's the problem?" I asked Nate, though of course I was beginning to suspect.

"Check out the olfactory dial," Nate said. He tapped on the dashboard, where one of the dials was displaying a running line of numbers. Just . . . numbers. And I couldn't even see them very well because there was a dinosaur sticker over part of it.

"Sorry," Nate said. "I like dinosaurs."

"Duh," I said. I would not trust a person who didn't like dinosaurs.

Nate said, "And I forget that most people can't read numbers. This readout shows the scent of Dà Hóng Páo."

"And that is . . . ?"

"It means 'big red robe.'"

"You know what you're doing? You're not making sense. Go ahead and give it another try."

"Dà Hóng Páo is an incredibly expensive type of tea. Like, tens of thousands of dollars per ounce. The statistical chance of someone simply standing on a street corner, drinking it, like that bearded man by the newspaper dispenser is doing, is—"

"Less than zero, I'd say."

"Well, no. You can't have a statistical chance less than zero. That would violate mathematical probability from the almost never to the almost surely fixed positive—"

"Nate. I was making a point, not a math problem."

"Oh. Well, then, *my* point is that we are almost certainly about to be attacked by the Red Death Tea Society."

"I am not in favor of that."

"I didn't think you would be. I calculated the probability was . . ." He paused here, smiled, and then said,

"... less than zero. Ha! See, *I* can make math jokes, too. Although, again, it's not mathematically possible to have a chance less than zero because—"

"Ahhhh!" I said, partially in exasperation with Nate, but mostly because of what happened next. A manhole cover whooshed about twenty feet in the air, where it floated in place while two men shot out of the hole as if they'd been fired from a moderately powerful cannon. One of them landed on the hood of our car. The second man landed right next to my window, and he immediately slapped some sort of peculiar machinery on the glass. It looked like a metallic octopus with robotic tentacles and an interior eye, staring in at me through the window.

"Huh?" I said. "Octopus?" I would have calculated my chances of suddenly facing a metallic octopus at . . . well, pretty low.

"Delphine Cooper," the octopus on my window said. The voice sounded like a robot's, which makes sense, being it was a robot octopus and all that.

"Hello?" I said.

"Don't listen to it!" Nate said. The man who had landed on our car hood had slapped another mechanical octopus on the windshield, right in front of Nate. "It's going to try to hypnotize you!"

"It is?" I said, and it was at that moment that the arms of the octopus, or the tentacles, or whatever you're supposed to call them, began to circle around its body. Just . . . spinning around. Around and around. I couldn't look away. It was fascinating. My mind felt fuzzy. Not warm fuzzy. But numb fuzzy.

"Tell me what you know!" the octopus said. It was awfully demanding for an octopus. I'd always pictured them as nicer. What's there to be angry about when you have eight arms? You could certainly get a lot of things done.

"Don't let it hypnotize you!" I heard Nate say, but his voice was distant. Muted and muddled. It sounded like when I take a bath and sink beneath the water. Even though I can still hear voices out in the hall or the television in the living room or the music coming from Steve's room, it sounds like all the noises are a hundred miles away and all I can really hear is the beating of my blood in my ears.

"Delphine?" I heard. It was the mechanical voice this time. I could hear it easily. "Tell me what you know." For some reason, this seemed like the most sensible thing to do, having a sociable talk with a robot octopus that was spinning its arms. So, I told it what I know.

"I know that friends are important," I said. "And that it's okay to be frightened of things if you don't let your fear stop you. And I know music makes me feel better, and that boys will always pretend they *let* you beat them in a race. I know that Steve has never found where I hid his favorite shoes after he told me I couldn't hang out with him and his friends anymore because I'm a girl. I know that I sometimes stay up all night, wondering what people think of me, wondering if I say the wrong things, wondering if I dress or act too weird, and wondering why I care about all these things so much. I know that—"

"Science," the octopus said. "I meant that you need to tell me what you know about *science*. All else is meaningless."

"I know that everything else *isn't* meaningless, because it's just as important to *live* as it is to *know*.

But, moving on, I'm not particularly good at math. That's a science, right? I also know that robots are cool. They're science. Is space a science? Dinosaurs? I know that Nate's dog talks, and if *that's* science, that's amazing. Are cakes and pies science? There's probably a scientific reason why some people prefer pie to cake. A strange mutation. It's unnatural."

"You don't know much about science, do you?"

"I'm sorry, Mr. Octopus. No. I don't. But in my defense—"

"What is a coordination compound?"

"Beats me."

"Describe the life cycle of a black hole."

"Life cycle?"

"What is complexity theory?"

"The theory that these questions are too complex for me?"

It was at that moment that I heard Nate's voice. Before, I'd been hearing it, but with that muted sound—distant, unimportant. Suddenly, he was as clear as if he was sitting right next to me, which would make sense, since he was. Even better, he spoke a sentence that, until he said it, I hadn't even come close to understanding how very much I wanted to hear.

He said, "Delphine, would you like to electrocute that robot octopus?"

"Yes," I answered. It was by far the easiest question I'd heard in the last few minutes. As soon as I answered, the glass of my window tinted almost to black, but there was a red spot about the size of my hand, and on it were the words "Press here."

I pressed there.

There was an immediate *zzzzackity-zack* sound, and our car was briefly surrounded by a burst of blue light, sort of like if the entire car had suddenly emitted a burst of electricity that fried all the circuitry in the mechanical octopus and made the members of the Red Death Tea Society use words considered *much* worse than "piffle," spilling the tea they'd been drinking and then shivering as the effects of the electrical burst made them spark and their hairs stand on end, and then they both fell over, totally unconscious. It was, in fact, *exactly* that type of a burst of light, because that's what happened.

People on the sidewalks were gasping in surprise, some of them moving quickly onward and others rooted to the spot. A woman on a motorcycle stopped and took off her neon-green helmet to see better, but then put it right back on, probably nervous about everything that was happening. One boy in his teens (wearing a Crimson Pterodactyls basketball jersey: *Go team!*) fell over when his dog ran around and around him, barking, accidentally wrapping the boy's legs tightly together with its leash. The boy fell over and the dog, a husky, starting barking at him with a query in his voice, as if the dog couldn't understand what was happening, making the two of us basically even.

Nate calmly drove forward, away from the unconscious cult members, driving beneath the manhole cover that was somehow and for some reason still hovering about twenty feet in the air.

"What the piffle was all that about?" I asked.

"They're confused by you," Nate said. "They can't understand that we're friends."

"Why is that so hard to understand?"

"Because all they really understand is science. And tea. Since we became friends, they think you must have immense scientific knowledge, or else there wouldn't be any reason why we'd hang out together. They can't understand that I just like being with you." He reached out and gave my hand a squeeze.

"You like being with me?" I said.

"Of course!" Nate said. His eyes darted around a bit. He looked nervous. He'd looked completely calm when we'd had assassins on our car. "You're funny. And you're . . . the way you . . . umm. I guess I . . . umm."

"Yes?" I said.

"It's remarkable," Nate said. "But I don't think I'm smart enough to express how you make me feel."

"Hmm," I said. "Nate, I could do without being attacked by giant cats or cult members, but, otherwise, I like being with you, too."

For the record, Nate blushed for the second time that day, and there was an icky stain on my window where the mechanical hypno-octopus had been stuck. These two facts are only related in one way.

Both of them made me say, "Hmm."

What's next?" I asked Nate. We were in Plove Park, having a picnic. Well, honestly, we were just eating a whole bunch of doughnuts, but it sounds less disgusting if I say we were having a picnic.

"We'll have to wait on Susan Heller," Nate said. "Which means on to Plan B: we'll scan the others. There's Vicky Ott, Jaime Huffman, Marigold Tina, and Kip Luppert." Nate looked at his phone and added, "I'm tracking Jaime Huffman right here in the park. He's on the other side, near the stream. Hey, are you going to eat that one?"

He was pointing to the last of the powdered strawberry-filled doughnuts. I *had* been going to eat it, but I'd already had two of them and there are limits, probably, to how many doughnuts I can eat. I pushed it closer to Nate.

I said, "I thought we had to scan Jaime's goldfish. Not Jaime. Wouldn't the goldfish be at his house?"

"Normally, yes," Nate said. He frowned. "Another anomaly, though. I'm tracking Jaime *and* his goldfish here at the park."

"That's strange. I don't know a lot of people who take their goldfish out for walks."

"No. Goldfish can't walk, anyway. Except for one time last year, on a Friday the thirteenth, when I temporarily gave legs to a goldfish."

"That's a story I'll admit interests me, but mostly I'm too terrified to know. Listen, I've been thinking, I have lots of friends, and they could help us. If we need to find all of these six messages of yours, wouldn't it be better to have several teams searching for them? I could call Liz. Stine. Ventura. Lots of people!" Because it was such a smart idea, I made the exact gesture that circus performers make when they somersault off the high wire to land in a cannon that shoots them up and over the tiger cage to land on an elephant's back, the gesture that acknowledges the thunderous roar of the applause.

"No," Nate said. He frowned, which is not the same thing as applause and *not at all* worth being shot out from a cannon.

"Why not?" I asked.

"Because if everyone knows about Proton and the Red Death Tea Society, it will cause too much panic."

"If you're worried about panic, perhaps you could *not* make giant cats? Just an observation, and . . . seriously, my friends are good at keeping secrets, or else we'd all be in detention every day, instead of usually just me. Anyway . . . we could tell them that it's just some scavenger hunt, although in that case we'd probably have to give a prize to the winners. Incidentally, I think it would be best if the prize was *cake*, since I plan on winning." I made my circus gesture again and stared meaningfully to the vast audience (meaning Nate) and waited for the applause.

"No," Nate said. Perhaps he was confused about applause?

"Gahh," I said. "Why not?"

"Dog nose," he said, which did not . . . in my mind . . . clear things up.

I said, "Did you know that your explanations always need explaining? What's this about dog noses?" Nate did a slow gulp. He put down the powdered strawberry-filled doughnut even though it was only half-eaten, which is practically a crime. His shoulders had hunched over and his lip was trembling. He looked like a circus performer who had somersaulted off the high wire and into a cannon that shot him almost, but *not quite*, over the tiger's cage, and was now trying to avoid engaging in conversation with a tiger that had not expected visitors.

"Nate," I said. "Talk to me."

"Dog noses," he said. "Remember when I smelled that you would be my friend?"

"You put on a mechanical dog nose and sniffed my arm, so, yeah . . . I kinda remember that."

"I can't tell you how happy I was. I don't . . . I don't really have friends. The science has never been right."

"I'm not science, Nate. Friends aren't science."

"Everything is science. Trust me."

"I do trust you, but that doesn't mean that even a genius can't be wrong. Maybe *life* is science, but *living* isn't science. It's not numbers."

"Maybe," Nate said, entirely unconvinced. "But what I do know is that other people would make me nervous."

"Okay," I said, also entirely unconvinced. Though, in a way, I did understand his anxiety. Nate's world was one of talking dogs, endless numbers, and giant cats, where my world was one of Liz and Stine and my other friends. Maybe Nate would need as much time to adjust to the thought of friends as I did to adjust to a giant cat?

Not that I'd adjusted.

In fact, I was entirely *not* adjusted, and I wanted to *un*-adjust the giant cat into being a normal cat, and it was time to do something about that.

I said, "So, shall we go find Jaime? Scan that goldfish? Make that formula?"

"Uh-oh," Nate said, looking past me. I grimaced. I have to tell you, I broke out into a sweat. I was starting to realize it's *never* a good thing when Nathan Bannister says uh-oh. When my mom says uh-oh, it's usually because she forgot to pick up something for supper, or because one of her clients is calling with a problem, or something like that. When Dad says uh-oh, it's usually because his favorite team lost the game in some horrendous (he thinks) or humorous (I think) way. When my best friend Liz Morris says uh-oh, it's usually because there's extra homework, or she stayed at my house for too long, or she accidentally sent a photo of her pretending to be a monkey to *everyone*, rather than to *me*, like she meant to do.

But I was starting to realize that when Nate says uh-oh, it's usually because something catastrophic is about to happen. Giant robots raging out of control. Or giant monsters raging out of control. Basically, giant things raging out of control.

"W-what's w-wrong?" I asked. Yes, I stuttered.

"Here comes Bosper," he answered. He pointed, and, sure enough, Bosper was chugging on over to us across the park, running as fast as his little terrier legs could carry him.

I said, "Oh. Whew. That's a relief!"

"Why?"

"Because I thought it was something bad."

"It *is* bad! Bosper would have *never* left home when he was supposed to be keeping an eye on Proton. This means Proton got away from him, and there's a giant cat raging out of control."

"Oh."

"Nate and girl!" Bosper said, charging up to us. I frowned, looking around to see if anyone else had heard Bosper speak. Nobody had. The nearest people were at least thirty yards away, practicing acrobatics. They were members of Penelope Spider's Vaudevillian Circus. They were yelling "Hep!" and "Ha!" and "Hee-yooo!" as they did their routines, so they couldn't possibly have heard the terrier's voice.

"What's wrong, Bosper?" Nate said as the dog came to a near-tumbling stop, huffing and panting.

"Cat on the street!" Bosper said.

Nate said, "Proton got away?"

"Bosper is not chewing on things!"

"Okay. Good," Nate said. "We've talked about that. But back to Proton—what happened?"

"Men with tea made lights that go *wooo-wooo*!"

"Hmm, I think I understand what you mean about men with tea, but . . . lights that go *wooo-wooo*?" Nate was confused. I was, too. Lights don't really do anything but shine. Unless . . . wait.

"Do you mean like a police car siren?" I asked. "Flashing lights and a siren? *Wooo-wooo?*"

"Is good!" Bosper said. "The Delphine girl is right! Car go by! *Wooo-wooo!*" He was jumping around in circles, overly excited in the manner of terriers. Then he made a sharp little noise from his rear. He immediately stopped jumping.

"Bosper farted," he said. The dog sounded sad.

"I do that all the time," I said. "Perfectly natural!" Bosper brightened up.

"There were men with tea?" Nate said, almost to himself, but the terrier immediately started racing around him, excitedly barking in agreement.

"And . . . they drove a car by the house?" Nate asked the dog. Bosper barked in reply.

"With sirens and lights going?" Nate asked. Bosper barked again.

"And Proton chased after it?" Nate said. This time, he really wasn't asking a question. He'd already figured out what had happened.

Now talking entirely to himself, Nate said, "Hmm. I'd calculated that the laser pointer would keep Proton occupied, but I hadn't factored the possible intrusion of other interesting light sources. The Red Death Tea Society played on Proton's natural curiosity to lure him from the house. And now, thanks to them, I've unleashed a giant cat on the city. Unfortunate. But an interesting problem."

"Yes," I told Nate. "An interesting problem." I tried not to squeak.

"Were humans eating doughnuts?" Bosper asked, sniffing at the bag.

"Help yourself," I said, watching Nate. He was deep in thought. I could almost see the gears turning in his head. Meanwhile, Bosper's entire head was in the doughnut bag and he was murmuring about lemon filling. Dang it. I hadn't known there was a lemon-filled doughnut. Now it was too late.

"We can't let the Red Death Tea Society get away with this," Nate said. "Forget about the formula for now. We have to save the town." His eyes fixed on mine. His

gaze was determined. He began to smile. I could see in Nate's eyes that he had devised a brilliant plan. Because he is a genius.

He said, "Delphine?"

"Yes?"

"Have you ever dressed up as a mouse?"

So, an hour later, I was dressed as a mouse. In the middle of a parking lot. Nate was on top of a grocery store but in contact with me via our cell phones. Bosper was sitting on the pavement next to me, looking alert and happy, wagging his tail. It was hot in my costume. I was nervous. I was practicing my mouse squeaks, which was not difficult to do because I was currently bait for a giant cat, and that made me feel . . . squeaky.

Luckily, the grocery store was closed for renovation, so there weren't very many people around. Just some boys skateboarding on the far side of the parking lot, trying tricks, frequently falling, occasionally taking photos of me. They waved a couple of times. I waved back. It never hurts to be friendly. It *would* hurt, though, to be eaten by a giant cat.

I mean, it would *have* to. Right?

I kicked a bottle along the pavement. It let out a little

of my tension, so I kicked whatever else I could find. A beat-up soda can. An empty egg carton.

Bosper made a sharp little noise.

"Bosper farted!" the dog said. "But that's okay!" He wagged his tail.

I said, "Can you sense Proton?"

"Maybe sometimes probably not!"

"Reassuring," I told him. It was difficult for me to see, because I was wearing my red goggles underneath the mouse head. Nate had felt bad about that, saying he hadn't ever thought to design a mouse costume that could detect invisible cats. A clear failing on his part.

"Run through this plan again?" I asked into my phone.

"I've been filling the air with the odor of catnip," Nate told me. I could barely see him atop the grocery store. He waved a hand. I waved a big mouse paw. There was an incense burner the size of a microwave oven in the middle of the parking lot.

He said, "Proton will be drawn by the scent, and then he'll see you. And he'll definitely want to pounce. I mean, what more could a giant cat want than a giant mouse?"

"And what more could I want than to be pounced on by a giant cat?"

"Really?"

"Umm. No. Nate, that was sarcasm. You really need to learn about it. What I was saying is . . . What's going to stop Proton from eating me? I mean, your plan better not be something about catching Proton while he's napping after his meal."

"Oh. I see what you mean. Don't worry, I have a string theory net."

"Which is?" Why did I even have to ask this question? Did Nate think I knew all about string theory nets? I looked down to Bosper and asked, "What's a string theory net?" He just started barking.

Nate said, "Oh. Well, the universe and all matter is composed of combinations of a certain substance. String theory says that these elementary particles are *not* zero-dimensional objects, but instead—"

"Hey, Nate? Kind of in a mouse costume here, waiting to be attacked by a giant cat. Can I get the abbreviated version?"

"Oh! Sure. Basically, my string theory net—"

"Which you have tested."

"Uh, so . . . basically my string theory net—"

"Basically your *extensively tested* string theory net, right?"

Nate said, "I've theoretically tested my string theory net, yes."

I sighed and told him to go on.

"Well," he said. "The net is based on the fundamental connection between elementary particles. I needed something really strong to trap Proton, and it would take the power of a thousand million suns to rip this net, because—"

"Good enough."

"Yeah. Because—"

"No, Nate. Good enough."

"Seriously, Delphine. You have to hear this, because it is positively *awesome*. In order to rip my net, you'd have to—"

"Do you want to put on the mouse costume?"

Nate said, "Uh, no."

"Then do what the mouse says. And, you know what? Now I know why it is that mice are always running around. I'm really nervous being a mouse."

Bosper, meanwhile, was still barking. I had to raise my voice, and it was difficult to hear Nate through the phone. I knelt down to the terrier and said, "Can you be quiet for a bit, Bosper? Nate and I are trying to talk."

"Okay, good dog!" Bosper said, wagging his tail. "But Bosper should be barking." With that said, Bosper (with obvious effort, and a frown) quit barking, and I went back to my phone conversation with Nate. I was telling him that as soon as I saw Proton I was going to run, and Nate was telling me how that was perfect, that I would lead Proton into the trap, and he was telling me where he'd set up the net, so that—

Wait a second.

I looked down to the terrier.

I said, "Bosper, *why* should you be barking?"

"Because cats are sneaking up!" he said.

I screamed something in return (it wasn't really a word, more just the noise a mouse makes when a cat is sneaking up on it) and I started running in circles. I dropped my phone into my back pocket and ran faster, because running faster was something I *really* wanted to do. Unfortunately, Olympic runners don't wear mouse costumes to a race. Why? Because they do not help.

"Where's the cat?" I yelled to Bosper, who was running alongside me in my sporadic circles. "I can't see anything in this ridiculous costume!"

"Everywhere!" Bosper said. It was not an answer I wanted to hear. Or one that I understood.

"No!" I said. "I mean, where's the cat?"

"Everywhere here comes cats!" Bosper said.

"Huh?" I said. "Cats? As in plural? As in more than one?" I stopped. I looked around. I adjusted my goggles and my costume so that I could see better. And there was a cat, a regular normal-size cat, strolling toward me across the parking lot. And another one. And there were several over by the grocery store. And there was another one that—

"Bosper smells three hundred and eleven cats." He paused, then excitedly added, "Three hundred and eleven is a prime number!"

I said, "Oh, good, math dog. I'm so happy I'm being stalked by a prime number of cats." I reached for my phone, which was *supposed* to be in my back pocket. The only problem was that mouse costumes don't *have* back pockets, meaning I'd dropped my phone somewhere in the parking lot. This was bad. I wanted to complain to Nate. Nobody had said anything about hundreds of cats. Still, they shouldn't be much trouble. I mean, just cats, right?

But. There were a lot of them.

I was watching them coming closer, ever closer, stalking me. All types and colors of cats, many of them with little jingling collars. Hundreds of tiny little bells ringing out. Hundreds of *predators*.

The boys with their skateboards were watching them. One of the boys skated away, rolling out onto the sidewalk and then disappearing into the distance.

He was gone.

I envied him.

The cats were coming closer.

"It's . . . just cats, right, Bosper?" I was looking to the terrier for some solace, hoping he would be better at it than Nate usually was.

"Bosper and the girl are in big trouble!" Bosper said. His tail was wagging. So much for solace.

"Should we run?" I asked the dog. Before I met Nate I considered myself very capable of taking care of myself. Now, I was dressed in a mouse costume and asking a terrier for advice. So there's that.

"Cats are good at hunting!" Bosper said. I think he meant that running was useless. His tail was still wagging.

I said, "Maybe you should start barking again?"

"Oh!" he said. "Bosper can?" There went his tail again.

"Yes, please."

Bosper began barking at the high pitch that terriers are so good at, as if they're tiny little opera singers hitting those high notes. The cats, as one (although, again, there were three hundred and eleven of them), stopped where they were. They considered the barks. Dogs, of course, are their natural enemies. And, lo and behold, here was a dog.

But . . .

I could see that in their tiny little feline heads they were doing some math. And, while I doubted there were any animals on earth better at math than Bosper, the cats were certainly smart enough to calculate that one dog is not equal in value (or in a fight) to three hundred and eleven cats.

So . . .

The cats started moving forward again. Padding closer and closer to me.

"I can see you!" I told the cats. Why were they *stalking*? Did they think they were sneaking up on me? And where was my phone? Maybe I could call Nate and yell at him and then he would find a solution to this new problem. Maybe there *wasn't* a solution. Either way, I could yell at him.

It was at that moment that Bosper attacked the cats.

Now, I guess it was because I was panicked, but I'd forgotten that Bosper was more than just a terrier who could speak and was good at math. He was a terrier who could speak, and was excellent at math, *and* he was Nate's dog.

That meant something.

He ran for the cats, and they moved out of the way, or at least they *thought* they moved out of the way. But Bosper was using the sonic leash, holding it in his mouth and flipping it around like a whip, using the sheer power of sound like a battering ram. I remembered Nate saying the sonic leash was similar to a force field, and also similar to a whip, which are two entirely different things. But one thing that the sonic leash *definitely* was, was *effective*. As Bosper neared the cats, they began flying up into the air as if launched by small explosions. In case you were wondering what it sounds like when three hundred and eleven cats are flung up into the air, I can't tell you. Sorry. It was too loud to hear anything.

I was still searching for my phone, and Bosper was still hurling cats into the air (his tail wagging so fast that it was nearly invisible) when the incense burner was suddenly crushed. It just . . . smashed down on itself.

Weird.

What could have done that?

Oh.

"Aha," I whispered. And then, "Oh, great."

I adjusted my goggles and found out I was right.

The answer was, of course, that a giant invisible cat had stepped on it.

"Phone!" I yelled. "Bosper! We need to find my phone! Right now! Proton is here! We need to tell Nate!"

"Find the phone!" Bosper yelled. "Good dog!"

I ran across the parking lot, constantly tripping, dodging cats, cursing myself for having lost the phone. I was also worried that I would spend the final moments of my life stumbling around a parking lot wearing a mouse costume, which is not how I want to be remembered.

"Who's a good boy?" Bosper yelled.

"Did you find my phone?" I yelled back. He was standing thirty feet away, wagging his tail, standing over my phone.

I said, "Yes! You *are* a good boy!" I went racing toward him.

"Girl has pretty smell!" the dog said. "Easy to find! Oranges!"

I said, "Oranges? Whatever, I'm just glad you—"

It was at that moment that the cats began to fall on me from the sky. Because what goes up must come down when the wielder of your sonic leash is distracted. The cats fell like rain. Or more like snow, because they were sticking to me, accumulating on me, covering me with a thick coat of angry cats.

It was neither convenient nor fashionable.

"Squeak," I squeaked. I didn't mean to. I was panicked. And I wasn't alone. The boys with their skateboards were yelling in surprise and confusion and several other emotions that boys have when cats are falling onto them. Two of the boys skated right into each other and fell down, and a wave of cats drifted over them. Luckily, they were able to break free of the feline horde and run away, largely because they were not encumbered by a mouse costume, like some people I could mention.

The boys were gone.

The cats were still falling from the air.

Bosper barked out, "Cat coming after you!"

"I know the cats are coming after me!" I said. "They're *on* me!" And they *were* on me, and they were scratching and biting and clawing and tearing at me, but I was semi-luckily in a mouse costume, and all they were doing was shredding it to pieces, so I was safe until I figured out how to deal with them. I hoped. I wasn't quite yet sure *how* to deal with them.

"Big cat is what Bosper means!" the terrier said. "Big cat is behind you!"

"Oh, you have *got* to be kidding!" My tombstone was going to read like a comedy routine. "Where is he?"

"Behind you!" Bosper said, which was no good at all, because I was once more running around in circles. Useless circles, I might add, because I had no idea where anything was. My goggles had twisted sideways, and there was a mouse costume over the goggles. And a layer of cats over the costume. I was in dire need of very specialized windshield wipers.

"Left! Right! Behind! Above!" Bosper was calling out Proton's position.

"Above?" I asked. What did he mean with *above*?

"Pouncing!" Bosper yelled.

I ducked and covered. Not my finest moment. Not *at all* the greatest defense against a pouncing giant cat.

I waited for impact. The normal-size cats were going

about their business of shredding my costume. I could hear Nate yelling at me through my phone. It was on the ground near me. I was still waiting for impact. A normal-size cat's paw came through my costume, just near my cheek. I reached up and tore the cat away. Tossed it aside. I was *still* waiting for impact. Just how long does it take a giant cat to pounce?

"He's got him!" I heard Nate say through my phone. I was still huddled on the pavement. Adjusting my goggles, I risked a peek. I looked in front of me. No giant cat. I looked behind me. Not there either. I looked to the left and to the right. I couldn't see Proton anywhere.

I looked up.

Well, there he was. No more than a foot above my head. His paws were stretched down toward me, reaching, clawing, struggling to grab me, but he was caught in midair by . . . something.

"Bosper?"

The terrier was standing at attention, head thrust forward, staring intently at Proton.

"What's happening?" I asked.

"Bad cat!" Bosper said. He did not look my way. He did not take his eyes off Proton. And he spoke through gritted teeth.

"Pick up the phone!" I heard Nate say. His voice was

coming from my phone. I grabbed it up from the parking lot and asked, "What's happening?"

Nate said, "Bosper caught Proton with the sonic leash. Proton won't be able to move."

I said, "That's great!"

Still on the phone, Nate said, "Unfortunately, it takes concentration to use the sonic leash, and Bosper won't be able to hold him for very long."

I said, "That's not great!"

"According to my calculations, we have roughly three hours before Bosper is too exhausted to keep Proton trapped."

Bosper, again without looking away from the giant cat that was caught in midair, said, "Three hours, forty-two minutes, twelve seconds, and then Bosper won't be a good boy anymore!"

"Let's go, Delphine!" Nate said. He'd hung up his phone and was running toward me across the parking lot. The normal-size cats were scattering away from him, running as fast as they could, all three hundred and eleven of them barreling off into the distance.

I said, "How did you do that?"

"Oh, I have anti-cat perfume. I wear it sometimes. Cats are creepy."

"They are not," I said. Then I thought about it and said, "Yes they are!" When you've been attacked by three hundred and eleven (three hundred and twelve, actually) cats while wearing a mouse costume, it changes one's perspective.

Nate pointed his cell phone at me and suddenly I was no longer wearing a mouse costume. I was just a sweaty girl in my normal clothes, standing in the middle of a parking lot, underneath a giant cat, reevaluating my life.

"How'd you do that?" I asked Nate.

"Costume disintegration ray. It was the fastest way to handle it. We have to hurry, because we still need to scan the other molecules and then create the shrinking visibility formula before Bosper's too exhausted to hold Proton anymore."

"Couldn't we just get that string theory net of yours ready? Put it beneath Proton and have Bosper drop him in?" Nate had taken my hand and we were running across the parking lot, leaving Bosper and Proton behind.

"Not advisable to use the net," Nate said. "I think the cats broke it."

"Broke it? How? Didn't you say it would take the power of a hundred thousand suns to break it?"

"Well, yes. Something like that. But when the cats were attacking you, I used the net to grab up a bunch of them."

I said, "I was wondering what you were doing." I was actually wondering more than that, but I thought best to leave it unsaid, as I'd been wondering if he was doing *anything* when the cats were attacking me. Anything *at all*. Except watching and laughing.

I said, "So, the net broke? How?"

"I had it calibrated for a giant cat. The smaller cats upset my calculations."

"They upset mine, too." We'd reached Nate's car. He slid behind the driver's seat and closed the door.

"Get in!" he said. "Hurry! The sooner we get this done, the better for Bosper!"

Right. The poor dog. I ran around to the other side of the car and leaped inside. As Nate and I sped away, I looked back to Proton, hanging in midair, spitting and hissing. And there was Bosper, below him, standing at attention.

"We'll be back soon," I whispered.

I wondered what else could go wrong.

So here's what else could go wrong.

Jaime Huffman was still in Plove Park when Nate and I returned. We'd parked the car on the street, raced across the park, and found Jaime. But he wasn't where he should have been. I mean, he was *exactly* where he was (walking across the park, looking pleased, and carrying an empty goldfish bowl), but according to Nate's tracking device the molecule we needed to scan was all the way across the park, at Black Stream.

We almost ran right past Jaime.

"Huh?" I said, pulling up short. I'd been focused on the grove of trees where the stream runs through.

"Oh, hi!" Jaime said. "What's up, Delphine?" Nate was looking at his scanner. Then up to Jaime. Back down to his scanner. He shook it a couple of times, like he was trying to fix some problem with the technology, which is something I guess even geniuses do.

"We're trying to save the city from a giant cat," I told Jaime.

He said, "Oh, cool." Jaime has long hair and wears button shirts with jeans. And he's tall. Almost six feet. I was mostly talking to his chest.

"So, what are you doing?" I asked. Nate was being no help at all. He just kept looking at the scanner on his phone, then over across the park toward the stream and the grove of trees. Then he would look over (and up) to Jaime, and restart the whole process, usually tapping on his phone's display screen at some point.

Jaime said, "Oh. I was setting Reginald free." He held up his goldfish bowl.

I said, "Reginald?"

Nate whispered, "Oh. Dang it."

Jaime said, "Reginald is my goldfish. Well, he *was* my goldfish. But I set him free."

"You . . . set him free?" I asked.

"Sure. It was weird. This morning, there were these two guys, and they knocked on my door and wanted to talk about goldfish." I nodded, as if two men knocking on a door and wanting to talk about goldfish is an everyday occurrence in my world. It isn't, but I wanted to keep Jaime talking. And *explaining*.

He said, "They came into my house and we had a good talk. They even made me tea. It was delicious." At this point, Nate made a strange grunt, but I frowned at him. We didn't want any interruptions. The quicker Jaime explained what he was talking about, the better.

Jaime said, "The men said they'd heard I had a goldfish, somehow. They said it was cruel to keep a wild creature in a small bowl, and that I should set him free." He paused, looked around and gestured to the park, then said, "It made perfect sense, so . . . here I am."

Nate whispered, "The molecule was on the goldfish. This is bad."

Jaime said, "I mean, can you imagine being trapped in something like this?" He held up the fishbowl. It wasn't very big.

I said, "It would be like being trapped in a mouse costume."

Jaime said, "Uh, yeah." He clearly wasn't convinced.

Nate said, "So you set your goldfish free in the stream?"

Jaime said, "Sure did."

Nate said, "That's . . . not really a goldfish's natural habitat. But, er, I'm sure he's fine. Anyway, Delphine and I really need to go!" He took my hand. Jaime raised an eyebrow.

As Nate and I raced off, Jaime called out, "Hey! Are you two dating?"

We were running too fast to give him the obvious answer.

Dating?

Pfff.

"He has to be around here!" Nate said. We were walking up and down the stream, exactly where the scanner said the goldfish *should* be. But, no, nothing.

"I still don't know why you put the molecule on a goldfish," I said. I was moving clumps of grass away from the stream's edge, looking behind rocks, looking everywhere.

Nate said, "I put the molecule on a goldfish because it was a not-so-smart thing to do. Remember, I'm supposed to do three dumb things every Friday the thirteenth!"

"Either your definition of not-so-smart is different from mine, or else you're not good at counting to three. Just today, I've uncovered evidence of you doing, like, seventy scrillion ridiculous things."

"Scrillion is not a number."

"Should be. Where do goldfish hide? Why isn't it here?"

"I'm not sure! Neat!"

"What's neat?" I was sifting through the soil at the bottom of the stream, pushing my hand into the sand and rocks and lifting them up. I was fairly certain that goldfish do not burrow, but I'm no expert in the matter. I was, however, an expert in having wet shoes, wet socks, and wet feet.

"It's neat not knowing things," Nate said. "It's like an adventure."

"We're fighting a giant cat and you're still looking for more adventure?"

"Adventures are like numbers," Nate said. "There's always a bigger one."

"Fantastic. But, mathematically speaking, there's only one Delphine Cooper, and I don't want her to be subtracted."

"Ooo," Nate said. "Awesome math reference."

"Thanks. I try to be entertaining. So, did it sound to you like Jaime had a visit from the Red Death Tea Society?"

"The goldfish men? You caught that, too? It was definitely them."

"Why would they convince Jaime to set his goldfish free?"

"Because of Frankenstein," Nate said.

"No idea what you're talking about."

"It was a book where—"

"I know what Frankenstein is, Nate. I just don't know why you brought him up. Unless—don't tell me you made a Frankenstein monster, did you?" I tried to picture Nate as a mad scientist creating monsters in a laboratory, cackling maniacally while lightning slashed across the skies. It was uncomfortably easy to do.

"Nothing like that," Nate said. "What I mean is, Maculte, the leader of the Red Death Tea Society, would like nothing more than to see me destroyed by my own creation, like Victor Frankenstein in the novel."

"So, this Maculte guy thinks it would be funny if you were gobbled up by Proton?"

"Not *funny*, exactly. Maculte doesn't really have a sense of humor. He just thinks it would be satisfying. Also, he loves creating chaos, and this way he can kill two birds with one stone."

"Or two sixth graders with one giant cat. Is the Red Death Tea Society really all that dangerous? I mean, what else have they done? What would happen if they took over the world? How come I haven't heard about them before? The first I really knew of them was when they stuck that hypnotic octopus on the car window and . . . OH!"

"What?"

"Hypnoctopus! That's what I should have been calling it. *Hypnoctopus*." I was a little disappointed in myself. I should have thought of that word right away.

"Nice," Nate said. "But the reason you haven't heard of the cult is because I've been stopping them, for the most part. Me, and others like me. Still, they were responsible for the Voluptuous Balloon Attack in Madrid, and the Invisible Oink Incident, with that herd of warthogs that nearly took over London, and for a time in the 1980s they managed to replace all the cats in Des Moines, Iowa, with robot doubles. There's probably still a few of them left." Nate was walking along with me, holding up his scanning device, tracking the molecule. I was still slogging along in the stream, looking for a gold-fish. I'd never before realized how good they are at hiding. Mostly, I see them in fishbowls, where there's not much in the way of prime hiding spots.

"There are robot cats in Iowa?" I asked.

"Sure," Nate said, with the most minimal of shrugs, as if the thought of robot cats created by a society of assassins was just the way things are, barely worth mentioning. It made me wonder what *other* things hadn't been mentioned.

"Why would the Red Death Tea Society make a bunch of robot cats?" I asked.

"Spies," Nate said. Again with the shrug. *Of course* the cats were spies.

"Some plot to take over the world?" I asked. "Or destroy the city, plunging it into darkness and despair and that sort of thing?"

"No. They were searching for a tea recipe. A master tea-maker used to live in Des Moines. Well, she did before the Boomerang Ape Event. There was an orang-utan that Maculte taught how to throw boomerangs so that—"

"There was a Boomerang Orangutan and you didn't ever think to call it the Boomerangutan Event?"

"Uh, no."

"That's weird, Nate. That one's really obvious."

"I suppose," he said, then, "Hey! It's moving!" He was looking at his scanner.

"The goldfish is moving?" I said, looking all over the area of the stream where the scanner was *promising* the goldfish was. "Then why can't we see it?"

"Not sure. Unless . . ." His voice faded off. He sounded troubled. And that was troubling.

"Unless *what*?" I asked. "And do not ask me to dress up like a goldfish in order to lure Jaime's goldfish out of hiding. For one thing, I'm not submersible. For another thing, the stream is cold. And third, no."

Nate said, "I'm worried the stream might have washed the molecule off the goldfish. I certainly hadn't planned on the goldfish being in a current like this. So we're not really looking for a goldfish, we're . . ." His voice faded off again. It was even more troubling than the first time.

I said, "So, we're looking for a molecule in a stream?"

"Maybe. Probably. Chances are. Yes."

"You realize that's significantly harder than looking for a needle in a haystack?"

"Considerably!" His face lit up. He was about to talk math. "The proportionate odds are—"

"Not now, Nate. How should we do this?"

"Oh, hmm." He frowned. He reached into his shirt and brought out a small technological device (it looked like a thick wire with beeping lights) and considered it, then put it back in his shirt. He took out another strange gadget (it looked like a tiny cheese grater with wires sticking out) and shook his head. He put it back in his shirt. Then he pulled out what looked like a tiny barbell, two small spheres with a bar connecting them, about five inches long. One of the spheres was entirely see-through and the other was pitch black. It started to hum. Nate frowned, then put it back in his shirt.

"Um, do *you* have any ideas?" he said. He was looking at me. The genius was looking at *me*.

So now what?

There were two hours and fifty-six minutes left before Bosper couldn't hold Proton anymore, and then a giant cat would begin rampaging across Polt. I knew exactly how much time was left because I was looking at Nate's souped-up cell phone. It showed the remaining time, counting down. And it showed a small blip that was moving away from Black Stream, moving in jerky movements. It looked like it was going . . . right past our feet.

I looked down.

It was a toad.

"Catch that toad!" I yelled at the top of my lungs.

"Huh?" Nate said.

"Look at your scanner! The molecule is on that toad somehow!"

"You're right!" he said, looking at his phone. "It must have washed off the goldfish and now it's on the toad! Catch him!"

I was quite lax concerning knowledge about goldfish,

but I do know three things about toads. One, they are quite slimy. Two, they jump weird. Three, they do not appear to enjoy being caught by humans. In fact, they do their very best to avoid being caught at all, and in doing so they employ their two main skills, that of jumping weird and being slimy.

Every time Nate and I would try to pick it up, it would jump away.

Every time Nate and I actually managed to grab it, it would slime its way out of our grasp.

And every time Nate and I dived for it, the toad jumped out of the way, resulting in an unending series of Nate/Delphine belly flops. Totaled up, it meant my clothes were stained and my shoes were soaked and my hands were slimy.

"Errrgh!" I said. "It's so slimy!"

"Actually, it's not. Frogs are slimy, but toads aren't. He might be wet from the stream, but toads, in fact, are—"

"If a girl helps a boy fight a giant cat, and she says toads are slimy, do you know what the boy should do?"

"Um. Just agree?"

"Good answer, genius." He smiled an apology. I'd made him nervous. I forgot how little he probably knew about girls. We aren't math.

"There it is!" Nate said. "There's the, uh, slimy toad! Right there!" He was pointing maniacally.

"I know!" I said. I was a little exasperated. What would Bosper say if he knew that Nate and I were having such trouble catching a toad, while *he'd* caught a giant cat? We were really failing. And really slimy.

"I got him!" I said, leaping for the toad.

"I'll get him!" Nate said, as he also leaped for the toad.

So, the thing is, Nate and I both dived for the toad. We smacked our heads together, and I knocked him out. Cold.

"Seriously?" I said, looking down at the unconscious genius. The toad was using the distraction to hop madly away, heading back for the stream.

"Stop!" I told it. The toad did not stop.

"Wait here!" I told Nate, who, being unconscious, did wait right where I told him as I dashed off after the toad.

I raced a few feet past the toad and cut off its path to the stream. Now, all I had to do was catch it, but that hadn't worked before, so I needed a new plan. Maybe I wasn't as smart as Nate and didn't know how to build molecular scanners or string theory nets, but I *was* the only one *conscious*, so I had to do something. I looked around the park. There was a couple in their mid-twenties playing catch. There was an old man flying a box-shaped kite. There were three squirrels skittering up and down trees, chasing each other. There were trees, a lot of grass, and there was a stream and park benches and a garbage can, but there was nothing that screamed *"toad catcher."*

Maybe I could borrow the old man's kite string and make some sort of toad lasso that could—

Wait.

Yes! The garbage can! There had to be something inside that I could use to catch the toad.

I quickly rooted around in the garbage can. Yes, me, Delphine Cooper, was diving into the remains of picnic lunches, soggy newspapers, and so on. Living the dream.

"Chinese takeout," I said, holding up a couple of boxes. Not good unless I could get the toad to overeat, making it so slow that I could catch it.

"Chopsticks," I considered, and then dismissed them, remembering how I'd launched a piece of sushi across a restaurant last time I'd tried to use them.

"Newspapers," I said, tossing them aside. They were no good. Unfortunately, I doubted the toad could read.

"Coffee cup, coffee cup, coffee cup," I said, sorting through the garbage. There were lots of coffee cups. And they were less than no good. The last thing I wanted to do was coax the toad into drinking some coffee, because that would only make it more excitable.

"Plastic bag," I said, tossing it aside. I didn't really have any use for a—

"Plastic bag!" I said, grabbing it again. It was perfect. It was full of a takeout meal, but I shook a half-eaten sandwich and a water bottle and bits of cherry pie into the garbage can and then raced back to the toad, brandishing the bag, feeling like I was a Roman gladiator facing off against a lion, though of course I'm actually a sixth grader at Polt Middle School and I was fighting a toad with a plastic bag.

"Ha!" I said, scaring the toad. I did this on purpose.

It leaped into the air.

I put the bag under it.

It slid inside with a *thlooop*-ing sound.

I held the bag up to the skies in triumph.

"You are caught!" I shouted. No Roman gladiator ever looked quite as dynamic and imposing as I did.

The toad (I had decided to name him Timmy) was secure in the bag. I tied it shut (making sure there were air holes) and ran back to Nate. We needed to hurry, as there were only two hours and forty-five minutes left before Bosper couldn't hold Proton anymore.

"Wake up, Nate," I said. He didn't.

I said, "Nate, wake up!" He still didn't.

"Nate?" I nudged him with a toe. "You okay?" He moaned. But he did not wake up. I noticed there was a bruise on his forehead. The old man with the kite looked over at us, making sure everything was okay. I gave him a thumbs-up to show that everything was fine, and he smiled and waved in reply, proving that he did not have a lie detector.

"Nate?" I said, my attention returning to the unconscious genius.

I nudged him again, a bit harder this time, and his phone started ringing and I fell over backward onto my butt, because at first I suspected that I'd triggered some self-destruct device when I nudged Nate.

"Ah, phone," I said in relief. On reflex, I grabbed his phone and answered it.

"Ahh, phone," I said again, still out of reflex, and this time much more embarrassing.

"Excuse me?" the woman on the other end of the phone said, obviously perplexed. "Is Nate there?"

"He is," I said.

"Oh. Could you put him on? This is Maryrose. His mother."

"That's great," I said, because apparently I wasn't finished embarrassing myself. I wiped a bit of sweat from my forehead and tried to think of what to do. I looked down to Nate. I nudged him with a toe. He was still unconscious. He was very good at it.

I said, "Nate's busy right now. He's . . . doing math." Would that work? It was the only thing I could think of. It sounded better than "Nate made a monster and we're fighting it, but I accidentally knocked your son unconscious and now it's just me and a toad."

"Oh, Nate and his math," Maryrose said. I could hear a lot of pride in her voice. Maybe a touch of exasperation. "Well, could you tell him that his father and I won't be home until later on Monday? He's found another cliff he wants to scale. And . . . is this Delphine?"

"Yes?" I said, as if I was unsure, but mostly I wasn't sure how she'd known it was me.

"Nate said you might be stopping by. Try to get him out of the house, will you?"

"I'll do that!" I said.

"We should have you over for dinner sometime."

"That would be great," I said, and I stopped my sentence right there, again because it sounded better than "That would be great, IF the city isn't destroyed by a giant cat, which is currently looking probable."

"Okay, 'bye!" she said.

"'Bye!" I said, and then we disconnected and I nudged Nate with my toe again, a nudge that was verging on being a kick, because there were only two hours and forty-three minutes to go.

He didn't react.

"Please, Nate! Get up!" Timmy the Toad was staring at me through the plastic bag. His eyes were accusing. I suppose he felt that I'd trapped him in the bag for nothing. He shook his toad head at me and then started licking a smear of cherry pie off the inside of the bag.

"*C'mon*, Nate!" I yelled. I shook him. I pinched his arm. I even slapped his face a little, like they do in the movies, which I'm fully aware is not a proper medical procedure, but I was frantic.

"Ooo, water!" I said. I needed to splash water in Nate's face. Now, how to do it? I did have the stream, but I didn't have anything to hold water (besides the plastic bag, which was toad-occupied) and so how could I—

Of course!

"Hello, again!" I told the coffee cups from the garbage. I grabbed three of them, poured the remaining coffee in the grass, and then filled them up with stream water before racing back to Nate.

I poured a cup of water on him. Just onto his chest. I was trying to be nice.

Nate only groaned and rolled over. I held the two other cups against my stomach and nudged him back into position for my second volley.

This time, I didn't hold back. Both cups. Right in the face.

"Hee-gahh!" he approximately said, sputtering and coughing and spitting. He shook his head. He looked around. Water was dripping off his nose.

"What happened?" he asked.

I said, "You dived for the toad and hit your head." No reason to go into any details about *what* he'd hit his head on. No time for that, either.

"I caught Timmy," I said.

"Timmy?"

"He's the toad. I caught him." I was holding the plastic bag, practically shoving it at Nate.

"You're magnificent!" Nate said, which verified that he is, indeed, a genius. Seriously, I'd begun to wonder.

Nate used his scanner on the toad, and more of those numbers appeared on the readout. They meant nothing to me. Just numbers, letters, and a few more of those squiggles.

"Make any sense yet?" I asked Nate.

"A little," he said, but he was very hesitant. "It reminds me of something, but I just can't quite understand. We need to scan those other molecules." Piffle. I was hoping we could skip some steps.

I released the toad and told it I was sorry for everything, but my apology was abrupt. Nate and I needed to go. After all, time was running out.

I could almost hear the ticking.

My phone beeped just as we were getting into the car.

It was a text from my best friend, Liz Morris.

She'd sent me an image of . . . a bag of tea?

The only thing in the message besides the bag of tea (which seemed to be about the size of a soda can and was bright red with "Red Tea" in black letters and some sort of strange circle around the letters) was a long row of question marks.

I texted Liz back, saying, What's this?

She texted back, Exactly.

I sent her a two-second video of me shrugging in confusion.

Liz then sent me a three-second video of her shrugging in a bewildered fashion.

I called her and said, "Liz, what's with the tea?"

"First of all, where are you?"

"Plove Park. The land of slimy toads."

"Are toads slimy? I thought that was eels. Anyway, why did you send me this tea?"

"I didn't," I told her. I looked over to Nate. He had a magnifying glass in his hands and was looking at some equations on his pants, writing more numbers on them and mumbling about binary modeling, which I suspected didn't have anything to do with fashion.

"Weird," Liz said. "I found the tea on my porch, and there was a card that said it came from you. But I wondered."

"Why?"

"What's my birthday?"

"July fifteenth," I said. Nate, not really paying me any real attention, nevertheless mumbled, "Hmm. Yes. Fifteen. That could work. At least reverse transgressionally."

Liz said, "Right. That's my birthday. But the card said 'Happy Birthday' on it. I didn't think you'd forget."

"I wouldn't," I said. "Did you drink any of the tea?"

"Ick. No. Why would I do that? It's tea. Are you coming over tonight?" I looked to Nate and thought of Bosper holding on to the sonic leash. I thought of the damage Proton could do if he got loose and rampaged through Polt, because that's what giant creatures do. They absolutely rampage. It's in their nature, I guess.

"Doubt it," I said. "I'm with Nate Bannister. We're fighting a giant cat." I would never lie to Liz, because friends should never do that to each other, and also because of a certain vow we've made that if we lie to each other we can't eat any cake or pie for a month, the thought of which sends shivers down my spine and makes my stomach jiggle nervously.

"You're with Nate?" Liz asked.

I said, "Yes."

There was a pause.

Then Liz said, "Nice."

And she hung up.

Before I could put my phone away, I got a text from my brother, Steve, wondering why I'd sent him some tea. I texted back that I hadn't. And then I got a text from Stine

Keykendall, wondering why I'd sent *her* tea. And then Ventura León texted to thank me for the tea. And I got a "thank you" text from Mrs. Isaacson, my homeroom teacher, and then I got a three-second video from Liz of her winking while holding up a piece of paper with "Nate" written on it, and then I got a gushing text from Tommy Brilp, who's had a crush on me ever since I can remember. He assured me he loved the tea and was drinking several cups of it.

I texted back, I didn't send any tea. I thought about adding more than that, but I couldn't think of what else to say, so I just put my phone away, wishing I could convince Nate that it was okay to tell my friends the truth. But I could hardly convince Nate to trust *other* people if *I* went behind his back and recruited Liz and Ventura and the others to the task of finding the parts of the formula that Nate had hidden all over Polt. I suppose in one way, I understood why he was acting like this—his shyness about grabbing more of our classmates. After all, *they* always ignored him in school. They never talked to him. Never invited him to anything. They didn't even say *hello* in the halls. So why should he trust them now? That said, trust is a two-way street, and until Nate understood that friendship *isn't* about science, it would be hard for others to trust him, too. And I wasn't completely sure if I wanted to involve Liz, anyway. What if it went wrong?

Nate asked me why I was sitting so quietly when—according to him—I charted in the upper-ninety-sixth percentile of people who like to speak their minds, no matter what. I suppose that means that this was one of those four-percent times, because all I could think of were the warning signs of my friends becoming involved with the Red Death Tea Society. The cult was clearly letting me know that they knew who my friends and family were, where they lived, and so on. And while I am generally considered reckless (I would probably rank in the upper-one-hundredth percentile), it's one thing to put myself in danger and another thing to involve everyone else I knew, especially if they didn't happen to have an incredibly smart genius handy.

So, for a few moments I squirmed in my seat, thinking of the world's deadliest assassins putting those bags of tea on all those porches, and knocking on all those doors.

"They'll be okay," Nate said. He reached over and squeezed my hand. I guess he probably knew what I was thinking. Probably had charts. Mathematical predictions. Maybe he could even read minds. If so, then he could see that I was thinking of a terrier in a parking lot who was struggling to keep a giant cat from escaping, much like the way time was escaping from me.

"We should get going," I told Nate. "Four more formula codes to go."

And he started the car.

chapter
6

Forty minutes later I was at the Polt Zoo where Kip Luppert was supposed to be working. However, I was not looking at Kip.

To be precise, I was looking at a hippopotamus.

To be even more and quite unfortunately precise, I was looking at a hippopotamus from *inside* its pen, from only about five feet away.

This was not where I wanted to be.

A hippo is one of the most dangerous creatures in existence. Its mouth is large enough to swallow precisely two and a half Delphine Coopers whole. They have hideous breath and horrible tempers. And nothing short of an elephant or a superhero has more muscle. Unfortunately, there were no superheroes along with me in the enclosure. There was just me. With my shaking knees. And with three hippos. Three big mouths. Three dreadful tempers. And one shirt that Kip Luppert had stupidly left behind.

Nate and I had raced to the zoo to find that Kip wasn't at his usual station, handing out program guides for the Daily Soar, an event where the zoo's mascot, an eagle named Baron Feathers, would start at the back of an auditorium and fly over the amazed audience to the stage below and the waiting arm—and offered fish—of its trainer.

"Where is Kip?" Nate said. "He's supposed to be here. He has a *schedule*." If you want to irritate a genius, do something off the schedule.

Through a hurried series of investigations we were able to discover that Kip had been asked to help catch some loose rabbits near the petting zoo, and that he'd then gone on break, but his break had been cut short when he'd been called to help out with the giraffes, and as the minutes were relentlessly ticking by we'd discovered that Kip had helped deliver bales of food to the hippos (seriously, actual *bales* of food for three hippos, and Dad yells at *me* if I have too many cookies before dinner), and then Kip had gone home for the day, but then Nate's scanner picked up a reading and . . . *beep beep beep* . . . it was coming from the hippo enclosure.

There was an official zoo volunteer shirt hanging from a low branch next to the bales of food.

It was Kip's shirt.

He'd taken it off while working and then simply forgotten it. The molecule must have gotten onto it, somehow. That was lucky for us. Nate and I stood at the edge of the enclosure looking at the shirt. There was a fence that went up to my waist, and then a twenty-foot drop to a moat, and then an island where the hippos were lounging. The shirt was there, on the island, with them.

"One of us needs to get that," Nate said. As he spoke, the closest of the hippos looked up at me. I'm not especially talented at reading hippo expressions. Not enough practice. Some things are obvious, though, and the look that hippo gave me was, "I *dare* you."

I told Nate, "It's going to be me, isn't it?"

"Well, yes. It just makes sense. You're stronger and faster and better under pressure, and it doesn't take a genius to pick up a shirt."

"So, I'm doing this because I'm not as smart as you?"

"Because you're stronger and faster and better under pressure." Nate gulped as he spoke, which I believe illustrates that he is not good under pressure.

I sighed.

Another hippo looked up at me. I could almost hear it say, "I *double dare* you."

I told Nate, "Get out your shrink ray. Let's shrink those hippos. You do have a shrink ray, right?"

"Are you serious? Do you know how many scientific problems there are with a shrink ray?"

I said, "Millions, probably."

"Three that I haven't yet solved. And if I had a shrink ray, I would have used it by now."

"Right."

There were eighty-seven minutes left until Bosper was too tired to hold off Proton's rampage. I looked at the fence. A twenty-foot drop. A twenty-foot drop to a moat. A twenty-foot drop to three hippos, the last of which was looking up and clearly thinking, "Delphine Cooper, I *triple dog dare* you."

"Piffle!" I said, vaulting the fence.

I have to say that the first part of my plan went splendidly. I'd planned on falling twenty feet down into the water, and that's exactly what I did. Straight down, with no monkey business.

A few frogs panicked when I hit the water, which wasn't part of my plan, but wasn't any great interference. I did think it odd that I (at eighty-one pounds) was scaring the frogs when they were roommates with hippos (each of which, if my math is correct, weighed infinite pounds) but that was a discussion for another day. I had a more immediate problem.

"Urggh! *Slime!*" I said, surfacing from the water, which was full of slime, and now also full of Delphine Cooper.

"Oh, just . . . just yuck! *Yuck!*" My clothes were covered in slime. I was shaking it off my arms, trying to kick it free from my legs, wishing that I could do that thing dogs do when they shake their whole bodies. Maybe Bosper could teach me the trick. If we survived the day.

"Gross!" I said, stepping out of the water and onto the island. "This is the worst! It's in my hair! Just . . . *ewwww!*"

There were gasps of surprise from up above, where the crowd was gathered. There were *oohs* and *ahhs* and some murmurs of concern, such as I'm accustomed to hearing when tests are passed out in class, although in this case I was the only one being tested, and it's entirely possible that I'd failed the test when I'd let Nate convince me to jump into the exhibit.

"All part of the show!" I said, waving above. They applauded, which was nice, but I was still covered in slime, which was not nice, and then—

Something moved in front of me.

I could provide several hints as to what this moving object might have been—such as that it looked, smelled, and sounded like a hippopotamus—but I'll just save time and say it was a hippopotamus.

It said, "Runnnk!" The noise was a cross between that of a cow and a pig and a giant movie monster.

I said, "Eek!"

Nate yelled, "Get the shirt!"

"Get serious!" I yelled. I *wasn't* going to make any sudden moves. I wasn't sure about making *any* moves. For all I knew the hippos had grown attached to the shirt and wanted to keep it. And they definitely didn't want me in their pen.

"I'll use the friend ray!" Nate said. I looked back at him. He pulled one of his strange mechanisms out of his shirt. It looked like several metal pencils held together with rubber bands.

I said, "The . . . friend ray?!"

One of the hippos said, "Runnnk!"

Another one roared.

They both moved closer. The third hippo was rubbing his butt on one of the bales of food, not paying any attention to me. He was my favorite.

Nate said, "Yes! It's a ray that recalibrates moods. I should be able to use it to make the hippos friendly." He flipped a switch on the strange mechanism and it began to make a *glook glooook* sound and emit several colors in concentric circles.

I said, "What the piffle, Nate! You had a friend ray?"

"Uh, yes?" Nate said, as if *everyone* has a friend ray and it's so obvious that *why* would it even be a topic of conversation?

I asked, "When I was joking about the *shrink* ray, did it not occur to you to say that you had a *friend* ray?"

"Uh, no?"

I glared at him. I thought about telling him that he might have to use that ray on *me* if he kept doing dumb things. I was so mad that it was very possible I was emitting colors of my own. All reds. They would have *all* been reds.

"Is it working?" I asked, looking at the hippos, but before Nate could say anything the answer became obvious. The hippos began . . . smiling? I guess?

It was kind of like smiling, anyway. And all the tension was gone from them, even though it wasn't all gone from me, because to be honest a smiling hippo has a startling resemblance to a hippo that is about to eat me, so even though the three of them were now acting very friendly, I was moving as slowly as possible, taking baby steps, reaching out my hand toward the shirt, barely breathing, edging cautiously closer and closer, and . . .

"Oh, the heck with it," I said. "I'm never going to get this chance again." With that, I leaped up onto the back of the nearest hippo. I'll admit it was a rather impulsive thing to do, but I don't think it would have come as a surprise to Mom, Dad, Liz, or any of my other friends, or any of my teachers, etc., etc., etc.

"Look at me!" I yelled up to Nate. "I . . . am . . . riding . . . a . . . HIPPO! Isn't it *awesome*?"

"Yes," Nate said. He wasn't as enthusiastic as I thought he should've been. He had a friend who was riding a hippopotamus. Such things should be celebrated.

"We really need to get that shirt," Nate said. "Time is running out."

"True," I admitted. Bosper was depending on us. So was the entire city of Polt.

"Giddyap," I told the very friendly hippo, nudging it forward like the chubbiest of all horses. "I'll call you *Lightning*!"

Lightning ambled forward with a ponderous waddle, heading toward Kip's shirt, which was hanging from the branch. The other two hippos were giving Lightning looks that I could only surmise were that of jealousy, since he and I were going to be best friends forever. I felt very good about myself. I would've positively *wept* if I'd missed an opportunity to be the first sixth grader in Polt Middle School history to ride a hippopotamus. The day wasn't so bad after all. I reached out and grabbed the shirt.

"I've got the shirt!" I told Nate. I held it up in the

air. It was another moment of triumph for Delphine Cooper.

"Yes!" Nate said, pumping his fist.

And the friend ray shot out of his hand.

It arced high into the air.

Nate tried to catch it. He fumbled for it. The device *thunk*ed off the back of his hands, rebounded off his chest, smacked onto the top of the railing, and then . . .

. . . fell

. . . into the moat

. . . below.

Where it made a *fzzzzt* sound as it released a short, solitary burst of electricity, then sank beneath the water.

I said, "Nathan Bannister, did you just drop the friend ray into the water?" I spoke this all in one breath. One breath was all I had.

He said, "Yes."

Still on that one breath, I said, "Do you . . . have another one?"

He said, "No."

I said, "Okay." By then I was squeaking. I'd used up the last of my breath and was afraid to take another one.

My faithful steed, Lightning, looked back over his shoulder to where I was perched on his back.

He said, "Rrr-RUNK?" I'm just going to go ahead and say that it didn't sound friendly.

Nate said, "You should probably get out of there as fast as you can."

I said, "You think?"

And at that moment Lightning went a little crazy. He began trying to shake me off, an experience that I can only liken to being attacked by an enormous blob of vibrating jelly. I flopped forward and grabbed his ears and held on for all I was worth, and Lightning bucked and shivered and bellowed, and I was trying to remind him of all the really wonderful times we'd shared, and the other two hippos were rushing forward with their *Delphine-swallowing* mouths and their *Delphine-crushing* teeth, and I was not in a very good mood.

Lightning jumped into the water.

He submerged.

Hippos, incidentally, are very good under the water and you should never challenge one to a breath-holding contest.

I said, "Blllooorrble!" (I was trying to yell "Nate!" but it came out wrong.)

Lightning began rolling in the water, trying to shake me free. I let go of one of his ears and thumped him on the head. Amazingly, this did nothing to improve my predicament. Instead, Lightning was now trying to scrape me away on the sides of the pool or get me in a position to bite me or keep me under the water for so long that I drowned. None of these were options I favored. Lightning was worse than any bucking bronco I'd ever seen in any rodeo, and to add to all the frenetic moves he began to spin.

His tactic was very effective.

My hand began slipping off his ear.

I was *really* trying to hold on.

But . . . no. I lost my grip.

Thrown by Lightning's sheer force, I whooshed through the water, and even up and *out* of the water. I was in fact hurled way up into the air. Like a rocket. I went five feet into the air. Ten feet into the air. Fifteen feet. Even twenty.

And down below me was the waiting mouth of what was about to become the first *Delphine-Cooper-eating* hippopotamus in history. The glint in the creature's eyes was that of extreme satisfaction.

I began to fall.

I whispered, "Piffle."

Nate reached out from the railing and caught me.

I yelled, "Yay!"

He heaved backward and hauled me to safety.

In a quick second I was standing next to him, amazed at the turn of fate, happy to be alive, though not quite as happy to be so thoroughly covered in slime.

"Ha!" I yelled over the railing, down at Lightning, who looked supremely disappointed by this turn of events. I shook the shirt at him, then turned and hugged Nate and (quite impulsively) kissed him on the cheek.

"Yuck!" Nate said. This was not the reaction I expected.

"Yuck?" I said. "Seriously? Is my kiss that horrible? I mean, it's not like I slobbered or anything, and I—"

"Sixty-three minutes left!" Nate yelled, looking at his phone. "We have to go!" He grabbed Kip's shirt from me, squeezed out of my hug, and started running off. Then, about thirty feet in front of me, right next to the monkey exhibit, which was totally where he belonged, he stopped.

He said, "Oh, and Delphine?"

"What?" I said. I was irritable.

"I meant *yuck* because of the slime." He gestured to his clothes. "You covered me in slime."

"Oh." It was true. I'd covered him in slime when I hugged him. Oops.

Nate turned a bit red, then added, "The slime was gross but the kiss was okay." With that, he turned and began running for the car again. The monkeys were all clapping and hooting and howling at Nate. I ran past them, racing after my friend.

"We're not dating," I told the monkeys, just in case they were starting any rumors.

In the car, I said, "Nate. You made a friend ray."

"I'm sorry! I should have let you know right away."

"It's not that. I'm just wondering, how do you make a friend ray? What kind of . . . research did you do?"

"Oh," he said. He was looking down, and wouldn't meet my eyes.

"Oh?"

"You meant, what does someone like *me* know about having friends?"

"Yeah. I guess I did." I felt bad, but at the same time it was true, though not in the way he meant. I reached out and gave him a friendly punch in the shoulder, so he would know I wasn't making fun of him.

Nate said, "To tell the truth, I watched you. The way you make friends so easily, it's so amazing! People always like you, so I distilled the sound of your laugh, incorporated a mathematical formula based on the curvature of your smile, and the scent you wear when you're—"

"Nate, none of that means anything."

"Data always means something!" he said. His eyes were wide. I think I'd offended him, a little.

"That's the thing, though, Nate. It *doesn't*. Friends aren't friends because of any data. They're friends because of . . . being friendly. It's like how the hippos were only my friends *until* your ray gun thingy broke, and then they were mad. But real friends don't need bribes or ray guns or anything but friendship. You've been a dork like a hundred thousand times today, and we're still friends." I punched him in the shoulder again so he would know I liked him, and of course to let him know that he'd been a dork, like, a hundred thousand times.

"Thanks, Delphine," he said. And I do think he meant it. I really do think he was trying to understand what I was saying.

But he was also writing some more calculations on his pants, working out some ideas, and the word "friend" was circled several times, surrounded by numbers, and by mathematical symbols that I couldn't even begin to comprehend.

I thought about giving him another little punch on the shoulder, but I have a rule of punching boys no more than a hundred times in one day, and I was worried that I might run out too soon.

# chapter
# 7

Susan Heller was parachuting.

Of course she would be parachuting. She couldn't have been reading in the library or shopping in the mall like she was *supposed* to be, or having lunch at Popples, the burger place where your burgers pop out of a machine like a jack-in-the-box. No, she was skydiving, otherwise known as leaping out of an airplane at ten thousand feet with nothing but a hunk of cloth strapped to your back, which, when you think of it, is nothing more than a style of clothing, so you're falling from ten thousand feet with a modified T-shirt.

And we simply couldn't wait for her to land, not with Bosper struggling to hold Proton, not with time running out. We were going to have to go up and *get* her.

Way up in the sky.

"This is great!" Nate said, proving that he did not . . . to my mind . . . have any idea what he was talking about.

Looking at the time on my phone, hoping against hope, I said, "You're sure we can't just wait here on the ground for her to, um, fall down?"

"Parachute down. She won't be falling. Well, technically she will be, but it's a modified style of falling."

"I'll just stay here, then, and modify falling all the way into *not* doing it."

"Where's your sense of adventure?" Nate said, which shouldn't have worked, but it did, because, dang it . . . I *do* like to have adventures.

I said, "Okay. You win. Where do we get our parachutes?" I looked around. We were standing at the edge of an airfield.

"Oh, you and I won't need them," Nate said. "We'll just jump out."

I lost my sense of adventure.

"What about modifying our fall?" I said. My voice squeaked.

"You'll see! This will be great!" He ran off across the airport toward a small plane. Susan's own plane was already high up in the sky. We were in a field. A flat meadow with a dirt runway for small planes, where the Polt Parachuting Program was held. Three *P*'s.

I hurried to the bathroom. If I was going to be jumping out of an airplane without a parachute, I would need at least one *P* first.

You know that lurch when a plane takes off? The one where your stomach says, "Whoa, hey! Are you *absolutely* sure this is smart?" Well, I had that lurch in my stomach even before our plane took off. It superquadrupled when the plane actually *did* take off. It grew even more when we were gaining altitude, while Nate was doing some stretches as if we were about to enter some strange and exotic challenge, like the obstacle courses on the game shows, except in this case, once we stepped out of the plane, the only real obstacle was going to be the ground, and there would be no way to avoid it. So, yes, I'll admit I was tense. So tense, I actually shrieked when my phone rang.

It was Mom.

"Did you order some tea?" she asked.

"No. Why?"

"A package of tea arrived. Had your name on it. Are you okay? You sound tense."

"I'm absolutely fine and there's no reason to worry."

"That sounded suspicious, Delphine. What are you up to?"

"Jumping out of an airplane because of a giant cat." I decided to be honest, because I doubted she would believe me, and then later, if she ever found out I *was* telling the truth, I couldn't possibly be in trouble.

"Okay," she said, obviously and thankfully not believing me. "Home for dinner?"

I looked over to Nate. He was writing a series of calculations and symbols on the side of the plane, occasionally stepping back to consider what he'd written. I didn't understand the math of it, but I could understand the symbols.

There were an awful lot of arrows pointing *down*.

"I hope so," I told Mom.

"There's the plane, sir," said the pilot. He pointed ahead of us, maybe a half mile, to where Susan's plane was soaring high in the sky. We were level with it, meaning we were also soaring high in the sky, flying in a plane that could only seat four people. The plane was bright red and seemed to belong to Nate, which was interesting, because I'm impressed by Liz Morris's nice bicycle, and here was Nate with a *plane*. I mentioned how impressive it was to own a plane and Nate said it was one of the first he'd ever bought. So there's that.

I'd never been in such a small plane before. Whenever

I traveled with my family it was always on big jets, so it really didn't feel like we were up in the air. Now, in a very small plane, the sky was only three feet above my head. And it was also three feet to my right. And three feet to my left. And there was ten thousand feet of that sky below me.

"The wind is loud," I told Nate.

"It'll get louder when I open the door," Nate said. He pointed to a door. One that he was going to open. This is not an acceptable plan on a plane. I would go so far as to say it was unacceptable.

"Won't Proton's giant size just . . . revert back to normal?" I asked. I had very little hope of this.

"Yes."

"It *will*?" My eyes went to the closed door of the plane. *Ha! Won't be needing YOU, door!*

"But it would take almost five years," Nate said. "And in the meantime, Proton is too dangerous."

I scowled. I refused to look at the door of the plane, though I could seriously hear it laughing at me. Instead of looking at the door, I looked to the parachutes. They were on a hook on the side of the plane. In other words, we weren't *wearing* them.

I said, "So what's our plan here, Nate?"

He opened the door.

I said, "Uh, the plan?"

"Look!" he said. He was pointing to where we could see, in the distance, people parachuting out of Susan's plane. They were too far away for us to make out any individual identities. They were so very small in such a big sky.

Nate took a step toward the open door, through which the wind was indeed making much more noise than before. The wind was going *"Whooosh, whoosh, whoa, what are you doing, you can't be serious!"* Everything inside the plane was flapping and fluttering. The parachutes were banging against the bulkhead, struggling against the hooks as if wanting to be free.

I had to yell over the noise of the wind, asking, "What . . . is . . . the . . . *plan* . . . Nate?"

He took me by the hand. I looked down at our clasped fingers. I was really stressed out, and holding Nate's hand was giving me a certain level of comfort that—

He stepped out through the open door.

He was holding on to me.

Out I went.

You know that saying about how in space, nobody can hear you scream? Well, that's pretty much true for when you're ten thousand feet above the ground, too. It wasn't *entirely* true for me, though, because there *was* one person who could hear me scream. It was Nate. In fact, I was screaming right into his face, which is a perfectly acceptable thing to do when you're ten thousand feet in the air and falling with no parachute. Oh, excuse me. I didn't mean ten thousand feet. I meant *nine thousand eight hundred* feet. No. Nine thousand *five hundred*. Nine thousand *two hundred*. And so on.

I said, "Piffle."

Why oh why had we stepped out of the plane?

Nate, for his part, was supremely unconcerned. It was as if he stepped out of airplanes all the time. Maybe he did. Urrrgh! That would be just like him! The wind was ruffling his clothes and hair. It was tearing at mine. His arms and legs were spread like he was making a snow angel. I was tucked into a fetal position. I planned to stay that way.

"Put out your arms and legs like this!" Nate yelled at me. He swooped by me, then put out his arms and legs.

"Like a flying squirrel!" he said.

"I am not a squirrel!" I yelled back.

"Of course not! Squirrels have no memory. But you do. You remember that I have a plan."

"I actually don't remember that you have a plan, because you never told me! Which is why I'm going to die!"

Nate said, "Just wrap this around your arms and

legs!" He reached in back of his shirt, then pulled out what looked to be a roll of tinfoil.

Tinfoil.

Our plan was based on tinfoil.

Which is the substance that crazy people put on their heads.

I was supposed to put it on my arms and legs. Which is crazier.

I said, "Tinfoil?" In the time it took me to say "tinfoil" (which is one word, with only seven letters) I probably fell fifty feet through the sky.

"It's not tinfoil!" Nate said. That ate up maybe another hundred feet of falling.

"Then what is it?"

"It's antigravity cloth. I invented it!"

"What?"

"Just put it on your arms and legs!" Nate said. He swooped closer and started wrapping some of it around my leg. It felt warm. That was nice. The sky was very cold.

"Why couldn't we have put this on in the plane?" I asked.

"Because that wouldn't have been as much fun."

"I am not having fun!" This was another scream that only Nate heard. Well, maybe. We *were* getting much closer to the ground. And I certainly *was* loud.

"Almost done!" Nate said. He'd already wrapped some of it around my left leg, and was finishing up on my right.

"About to activate it," he said. "Get ready."

"I'm ready!" I can wholeheartedly confirm that I was ready.

Nate took out his phone and entered a couple of codes. His tongue stuck out as he concentrated. It was taking too long. We plummeted fifty feet. Another hundred. Two hundred more. I was not unconcerned with this.

I said, "Did you hear me say I was ready?" It's possible that I screamed it. I was probably frightening the birds, at least.

"Here!" Nate said, and then . . .

. . . whoop.

I was upside down.

Hanging in midair.

By my legs.

Not falling.

"Nate!" I yelled, but he was gone. He was falling below me, already a hundred feet gone. It was even more amazing to gauge the speed at which I'd been falling when I could see it in action. Nate was almost a speck already, plummeting to the ground. But, as he was disappearing, I could see him wrapping the antigravity cloth around his arms and legs.

I just watched the speck, hoping that he hadn't waited too long. If something happened to Nate, that would be horrible. Even though we had just become friends, I was already feeling like my world was expanding, like I was catching sight of a huge part of the world that I'd never known existed, like the world was much broader and far deeper than I'd ever suspected. So, if Nate was gone . . . it would have been terrible. Also, I'd spend the rest of my life hanging upside down, seven thousand feet in the air, hoping for cell phone reception and for somebody to believe me when I called them to say where I was and what I was doing, a hope that seemed unlikely.

I watched the speck that was Nate. It grew smaller. And smaller.

And then . . .

Bigger.

And bigger.

He came soaring back up, grinning. He hovered in the air in front of me, turning his head sideways so that he could see me better, since I was still upside down.

He said, "I came up with this idea a few Friday the thirteenths ago!"

"What?" I was enraged. "You came up with the idea to scare me to death a *few Friday the thirteenths* ago? You didn't even know me then!"

"Well, I had a dossier on you, of course. But that's not what I meant. I mean the idea to jump out of an airplane and test my antigravity cloth at the same time."

"Oh. Well, then—wait. *Test* the antigravity cloth? This stuff hasn't been *tested*?" I stared at the almost-tinfoil that was on my legs. I was back to screaming. It wasn't wise. All the blood was draining to my head and I was beginning to get dizzy.

"Of course it's been tested!" Nate said. "In theory. Hypothetically. The mathematical modeling definitely works. There was fully a ninety-eight percent chance of success!"

"I jumped out of an airplane—was *pulled* out of an airplane—with a two percent chance of *failure*?" I was glaring at Nate. You can go ahead and picture laser beams shooting out of my eyes, because there was at least a three percent chance of that actually happening.

"Your face is all red," Nate said.

"Isss cuzz mmm angry!" I said. My words were beginning to slur. I was quite dizzy.

"Oh!" Nate said. "You're upside down!" I just stared at him. I mean, seriously, the genius hadn't figured out that I was upside down? Nate truly *is* a genius, but that doesn't always make him smart.

He began wrapping pieces of the antigravity cloth around my arms. Soon, with their support, I was floating upright. It was much better than being upside down. My dizziness began to pass. The clouds were rolling by. The cloth around my arms and legs truly did look like tinfoil, but with a glistening sheen, like oil on water, reflecting a myriad of colors. It felt warm. And it was slightly humming.

And I was floating in the sky.

And it was awesome.

I said, "Nate, I . . . " My words trailed off. The two of us were together, soaring through the clouds. Flying. We could control our flight by waving our arms, kicking our feet. It was a little like swimming, if every swim stroke shot you three hundred feet forward. It was . . . amazing.

"Forgive me now?" Nate said, grinning.

"Not at all," I said, also grinning.

"Oh," he said, disappointed. And then, "Oh! We have to catch up with Susan!" He turned and we went zooming toward the distant specks of Susan and the other parachutists who had jumped from their own plane. We were traveling far faster than they were, even faster than we had been when we were falling, and certainly much faster than Susan, as she had her chute open and was simply floating through the sky.

The wind was hurting my eyes, drying them out. I slid through a cloud to get a little moisture. It felt like a strong fog.

"Put on your goggles," Nate said. He was putting on the same goggles we'd worn when we were looking for Proton. It made me worry there were other giant cats, giant *flying* cats, in the sky. Absurd, of course, but then Nate had certainly brought quite a few absurd things to light. In my defense, it must be remembered that I'd recently been dizzy.

"They'll help your eyes," Nate said, as I was putting

on my goggles. "And I'm going to bend a few light waves soon. This will help us see each other."

"You're going to what?" I asked.

"Bend light waves. An eye perceives objects by reflected light, but if light waves bend around the object, there will be nothing to report, no reflections. Even if the object exists, it will remain unseen."

I thought about this, digesting his words, trying to make sense of them.

I said, "Are you talking about making something invisible?"

"Yes. But technically it's—"

"Aargh. Just say *invisible*. I don't want a science lesson right now. I just want to soar through the skies and scare pigeons. And don't you have to scan the molecule on Susan's, uh, neck, or wherever you put it?"

"I do! That's why I'm bending light waves. So she won't notice us. I thought it might scare her if somebody flew up to her in the sky and touched a molecular scanner to her neck."

"Yeah."

"Stay here! Off I go!"

He started to zoom away.

I said, "Wait!"

He paused. In midair. Which looked really cool. Even though he doesn't dress very well.

He said, "What?"

"You're not invisible!" He smiled at this, and tapped at his goggles as a way of indicating mine. I understood what he meant, and so of course I knew what I would see when I took off my goggles. I saw . . . nothing. Nate had simply disappeared. I pulled my goggles back on and waved. He zoomed away.

He'd told me to wait for him, but in case I haven't made this clear I'm not very talented at doing what I'm told. You can ask my mom about that. Or Dad. Or any of my teachers, especially Mr. Marsh, my science teacher, who always repeats the steps of an experiment for me, and me alone, and says that he really does encourage my scientific explorations (he always pauses before saying "explorations") but that he wishes I would quit making so many things explode.

Anyway, I followed Nate.

He zoomed through the air, swimming, but fast. I kept up with him, staying about a hundred feet back, flapping my arms like a bird. Honestly, I actually felt like a bird. It was amazing to see the world as they do, to see the city and the countryside as a whole, instead of just a collection of streets, buildings, trees, and so on. Birds must revel in the majesty of the skies.

I do wish they wouldn't poop on everything, though.

Nate was closing in on Susan. She was doing a tandem

jump with her mother, so she was strapped to her mother's torso. Her mother was trying to calm Susan down, because she was a little afraid of what they were doing. How childish! You'd never hear *me* complaining about falling through the skies. Well, at least you *didn't* hear me, because there was no one but Nate around when I was complaining via a series of horrified screams.

Nate slowed down as he neared the two of them. He was a hundred feet away from them. Then fifty. He had his molecule reader out, ready to scan Susan at any moment.

And then he just stopped. Well, not exactly stopped, since he was flying through the air, consistently keeping about twenty feet away from Susan and her mom, who were parachuting down through space. The ground was only about a couple thousand feet below. *Time to get moving, Nate!*

But he wasn't. He wasn't doing anything. I couldn't understand what was happening. Had something gone wrong? Did he need help? He was just staring at her. Just . . . staring at her.

Oh.

I yelled, "Nate! Quit staring! She's pretty and all that, but we have a job to do!"

"Huh?" Nate said, apparently lost in a haze of Susan Heller–inspired idiocy. He had a big dreamy grin as he flapped in the air beside her, entirely invisible to her eyes (which he usually was anyway, if I might make that comment) and all but drooling as he marveled at her long brown hair and whatever else he found pretty about her. She has a good smile, I guess.

Except she wasn't smiling just then, as she was falling from the sky above the grounds of the Polt Parachuting Program. At first, she'd been horrified and grimacing. Then, for a few hundred feet, she'd actually seemed like she was enjoying it. Now she was frowning. And complaining.

"Mom," I could hear. "I wanted to go to the mall. I have shopping to do. Shopping." The last word, "shopping," was stretched out over two or three seconds, and perhaps a hundred feet of descent as they floated down through the skies among the other parachutists. Her voice was high, with a bit of a whine to it, and when she opened her mouth the rushing winds went barreling inside and puffed out her cheeks, making her sputter. Which made me laugh.

"I'm sorry you wanted to go shopping," her mother was telling her. "But the coupons from those strange men with tea were for free skydiving *today*. Today *only*. Don't you want to experience new adventures?"

"I don't want new adventures! I want new shoes!" I couldn't believe what I was hearing. Who doesn't want adventures? I would have traded all my shoes to be just where I was. Minus the impending giant-cat doom, of course. But time was running out. We were a few hundred feet above the ground. Actually, *only* a few hundred feet above the ground.

I said, "Nate! Scan her molecule!"

He looked back at me and said, "Oh. I wish she would smile." He made it sound like the first line of a poem, and I was not going to have that. I simply *wasn't*. So I zoomed closer to him, deciding that somebody better do something before time ran out. Obviously, I would have to take the initiative.

It was at that point when we had a little mistake. A tiny bit of a mishap. Some clumsiness. Nothing much to it. Happens all the time.

Here's what happened.

I zoomed forward to grab the slingshot so that I could scan for the secret message myself, but I did it at the same time Nate decided he needed to fly around to Susan's other side, I guess to admire her profile or whisper a poem into her ear or some stupid thing like that. Anyway, we collided.

With our heads.

There was a noise, like *CLUDDDK*.

And I sort of knocked Nate unconscious.

*Again*.

In my defense, it's not my fault that my skull is harder than his. Maybe all that thinking softens his head? The point is, I was stunned for a bit, no more than a second, and when my head cleared I could see that Nate was out cold.

And he fell.

So, you see the problem here, right? Normally when I accidentally knock a boy unconscious, the boy just tumbles to the hallway floor, or the ground, or the wooden floor of the gym, or that one time at the swimming pool when we needed Candy Crable, the lifeguard. So, see? No big deal.

But this was the first time I'd knocked out a boy when we were way up in the sky. About eight hundred feet, at that point.

I had to save him.

I dived as fast as I could, flapping my arms and kicking my feet and pretending I was a cheetah, which doesn't make a lot of sense. I mean, cheetahs *are* fast, but they do a lot better on the open plain than they do in the sky. Still, I was trying to *feel* fast, and a cheetah was the first thing I thought of.

"Cheetah!" I yelled, zooming down through the air. I was closing the gap. We were only a hundred feet apart. But the ground was only three hundred feet below us. Do you know what the ground looks like when you're falling? It looks *hard*. When you're walking on the ground it looks like just the ground, but when you're falling it looks *hard*.

I yelled, "Nate! Wake up!"

Nothing.

I was flapping my arms like crazy. Like *super*-crazy. We were only fifty feet apart. The ground was still a couple of hundred feet below.

I was going to make it!

Then the antigravity cloth tore away from my left arm and went whooshing up into the skies, mocking gravity, and mocking me. It immediately unbalanced me, sending me into a dizzying spin. I lost track of Nate.

One hundred and fifty feet to the ground. I didn't know what to do. I was starting to panic, but fought it off. I reached up and tore the tinfoil away from my right leg, hoping it would somewhat balance me so that I would quit spinning. It worked, but barely, and I wasn't moving nearly as fast anymore. I quickly looked around, hoping against hope that I wouldn't see Nate crumpled on the ground. I didn't see him on the ground, which was good, but I also didn't see him *anywhere*, which was bad. My throat was tight.

I didn't see him.

I didn't . . . *THERE*!

Nate was still limp. Unconscious. Plummeting. He was fifty feet from the ground and completely unable to control his antigravity cloth. I dived for him as fast as I could, but at an angle. My mind was screaming that I had to grab him immediately, as fast and as directly as possible, but it wouldn't have done us any good if we both slammed into the ground at full speed after I caught him. I had to come at him from the side, grab him before he could hit. Before *we* could hit.

He was forty feet from the ground. We were over a small rise at the edges of the open field. The hill was no more than thirty or forty feet tall. I could have *really* used another thirty feet of distance.

Nate was thirty feet from the ground. Then twenty, and then ten. I was reaching for him. Stretched out. We were nine feet from the ground. Eight. Seven.

I grabbed his ankle and held on tight.

I pulled up as hard as I could, trying to stop Nate's fall. I was wishing I'd done more weight lifting. I was wishing I'd done *any* weight lifting.

Nate's fingers touched the ground. I was holding him upside down. I was yelling. We scared a bunch of sparrows up from the ground and they took to the skies as if they could never ever fall.

"Aaaargh!" I wasn't really screaming. I was grunting with effort. Nate's fingers were kicking up dust as I dragged him along the ground, trying to stop his fall. And then . . .

. . . and then . . .

. . . we started to move higher up into the sky.

Five feet into the air.

Six feet into the air.

Seven feet into the air. We weren't exactly soaring.

Finally, we were about twenty feet into the air, and at that point I realized I wasn't in the mood for being in the air right then. So I landed.

I was on my feet. And it felt good. It felt *very* good to be standing on solid ground. Although, to be honest, Nate was rather heavy. He started to slide out of my arms and I had to hug him really tight. Which of course meant that he chose that time to wake up. I bet he did it on purpose.

"Delphine?" he said. He was dazed. His eyes were unfocused.

"Nate!" I said. I was really happy that he was alive. I thought I'd lost my friend. I think it was that moment when I started to realize how quickly he'd become important to me. I wanted to understand science. I wanted to understand Nate. I wanted to call Liz Morris and tell her about the expression on Nate's face when I'd kissed him on the cheek. I knew that Liz would make fun of me and I wanted that, too, in a way.

So I kept hugging Nate.

"What happened?" he said. His words were slurred.

"You smacked your head into mine," I said. I felt that it was best to put the blame where it almost assuredly and entirely more or less belonged. And, yes, I was still hugging him.

"I must have fallen," he said. "And . . . you caught me?" I nodded.

"Thank you," he said. His arm went around my back and he started to hug me in return. It was our first full hug. But of course we're only friends and so I'm only mentioning this for no reason in particular.

Nate looked into my eyes and said, "Delphine. I . . ." He stopped. Gulped. He was verbally stumbling. I was still hugging him. He said, "Delphine, I think that you're really—"

It was at that exact moment that Susan Heller and her mother fell on us.

In their defense, they couldn't have seen us, as Nate's light wave–bending was still going on, meaning we were invisible.

"Ooomph!" I said, at the moment of the quite dramatic impact.

"Guhhh!" Nate said.

"Aaaph!" Susan Heller said.

"Awwpp!" That was from Susan's mother. Nate and I went tumbling, and mother and daughter went sprawling, still bound together by their tandem parachuting harness. We all fell over. And then the parachute itself settled whimsically over us, trapping us together.

"What did we hit?" I heard from somewhere in the big nylon parachute that was covering us. It was Susan's mother.

"I hate parachuting!" I heard. That was from the brat.

"I have an idea," Nate said, whispering to me. He reached into his shirt and pulled out his electrical slingshot (of course I mean the molecular scanner, but you really do need to see the device, and then you'll understand why I call it a slingshot) and also another small machine. It was shaped like a cell phone.

"What's that?" I asked. I was keeping my voice down. The impact had wrecked Nate's light-bending machine, meaning we were no longer invisible, but we *were* hidden by all the parachute cloth, and I wanted to stay that way.

"An illusion machine. I'll project images so that you

and I will look like two deer. We have to do something now, since they know they hit *something*."

As Nate was speaking, two things were happening. The first was that he was reaching out and touching the slingshot to the back of Susan's neck as she crawled past us, having unhooked herself from the parachute harness, and now bitterly complaining about missing all the good sales at the mall. She never even felt it when Nate touched her neck. The molecule was scanned. Success! Three parts of the formula retrieved.

The second thing that was happening was that Susan's mom was gathering up the parachute, pulling it away from us, revealing our illusioned bodies. As soon as she did, Susan and her mother both gasped and stared. Nate and I stood very still.

Susan said, "Mom? Do you see them?" She pointed to us. Her eyes were wide.

"Y-yes," her mother said. She looked . . . scared? They *both* did. Why were they scared of *deer*?

"Bears!" they both screamed. Oh, wow, did they scream. Nate looked down at his device. He grimaced.

"Uh-oh," he said.

"Did you . . .?"

"Yeah. It's on the setting for bears. An honest mistake. It was dark underneath the parachute!"

"Bears!" Susan and her mother screamed again. "They're growling!"

"Do something!" I told Nate. I nudged him.

"They're attacking!" Susan yelled.

And then they ran.

Honestly, it was kind of funny. I didn't mind Susan running and screaming and I even secretly enjoyed how Susan tripped and fell at one point. Nate, of course, was heartbroken.

"Susan?" he said sadly, reaching out. His eyes were weepy. His lips were trembling. I rolled my eyes at him.

Boys.

Bears, too, I guess.

chapter 8

Betsy," Nate said. "Where are Vicky Ott and Marigold Tina?"

We were zooming along in Nate's car, driving past Krallman Forest, and he had apparently forgotten my name.

"How would I know where they are?" I asked. "Don't you have some . . . some *science* way to find them? And my name isn't *Betsy*. It's *Delphine*." I tried not to sound irritated, and I tried not to punch Nate in the arm. It's probable that I sounded irritated, though, and it's positive that I punched him in the arm.

"I know you're not named Betsy," he said, rubbing his arm. "I wasn't talking to you."

"Piffle," I said. "Nice try. But there's nobody else around, so that's the flimsiest excuse that—"

"Scanning for Vicky Ott and Marigold Tina," the car said. The voice was feminine and coming from the glove box. I opened it up and looked inside. There wasn't anybody inside. No weird robot car face, either. It was only a speaker. I was relieved. Though somewhat disappointed.

"That girl is looking in my glove box," the car said.

"Oh, Betsy doesn't like that," Nate said, gesturing for me to close the glove box. I did.

"Your dog and your car both talk," I said.

"Yeah. Listen, we spent too much time getting that molecule reading from Susan. Bosper can't hold Proton much longer, so one of us will have to go find Vicky Ott and the other will need to scan the molecule on Marigold Tina."

The glove box voice said, "Marigold Tina is at Bowen Science Center. Vicky Ott is traveling along Highway 36 at a speed of sixty-two miles per hour. She is three miles ahead of our current location."

"That's lucky!" Nate said. "Only three miles away!"

"Right! Drop me off, and then I'll go to the science center, and—"

"I know the science center better than you do, so I'll go there. You catch up with Vicky."

"Uh, Nate? That doesn't make any sense. I'm—"

Nate opened the car door. He touched a button on

his belt and simply stepped out of the moving car, accompanied by my screams.

He didn't fall.

He began hovering right next to the car, shooting along on several tiny jets that were whooshing from his belt.

"See you later!" he said, and then shot up into the sky and zoomed off over the horizon.

Leaving me sitting entirely alone in the passenger seat of his car.

I said, "Ahhh!" It was barely a squeak. The car was speeding down the highway.

I said, "*AHHHHHHHHH!*" It was about three levels above a shriek. The car was now absolutely roaring down the highway.

I rolled down my window, leaned outside, and screamed. "*AHHHHHH!*"

The car said, "'*AHHHHHH*' is not a command, Driver Delphine Cooper. Please enter a command."

"What?" I said, suddenly noticing how, despite the fact that nobody was behind the wheel, the car was traveling down the center of the proper lane at a reasonable speed.

The car said, "You are now in command of this vehicle. Do you wish to accelerate and overtake Vicky Ott?"

"Um, yes?"

"Noted," the car said. We began to drive a bit faster.

I said, "So you're some autopilot thing?"

The car said, "I am not a *thing*. I am Betsy."

"Oh. Hi, Betsy. Should I be in the driver's seat?"

"Unnecessary," Betsy said. "But it's your decision." We were passing several cars. Each of them, of course, had drivers.

I said, "Actually, it might be necessary. We can't have the other drivers thinking nobody is driving our car. It could cause a panic. Accidents."

Betsy said, "I am currently projecting an illusion of a driver."

"You are? What driver?"

"I have chosen to portray you, Driver Delphine Cooper, at fifty years of age."

"Really? Me? Fifty years old? I have to see that! Can I see that? Why can't I see that?" I moved my hand through where a driver would be seated.

"The illusion is triggered only by the window. You would have to be outside if you wished to see. Would you like to step outside?"

"Is it *safe* to step outside?" It did not sound safe to step outside. I did not, for instance, have a belt that came complete with several mini-jets. Yet.

Betsy said, "No, it is not safe for you to step outside. You would fall and be seriously injured."

I said, "I wouldn't like that." I was starting to detect a certain . . . tone in Betsy's voice.

"If you wish, I could describe the image of you at fifty years of age," Betsy said.

"Okay. Sure." I suspected what was coming.

"Scraggly gray hair. Drooping eyes. Wrinkles. Splotchy, thin skin that—"

"Betsy?"

"Yes, driver?"

"Are you mad at me for something?"

"I am not capable of being angry."

"Oh. That's a relief, because—"

"But if my programming *did* include emotions, then it *is* entirely feasible that your unnecessary and unwelcome intrusion into my association with Nathan Bannister, the mastermind of my creation, could trigger irritation, annoyance, aggravation, and similarly justified feelings."

"I see."

"Further, my sensors detect traces of your lipstick on Nathan's cheek. You have kissed him."

"What? I mean, I did, but I don't even *wear* lipstick! Why *would* I wear lipstick? Mom would kill me if I ever wore lipstick. So I don't. Except for a couple of times at Liz's house when we tried it on, but mostly I just wrote 'dork' on Liz's arm, and then it didn't wash off for three days, and she had to wear long-sleeved shirts and pretend she was sick during gym class, but none of that matters because I didn't wear lipstick when I was kissing Nate, and it was only a 'thank you for saving me from getting hippo-chomped' kiss on the cheek because, again, *not* romantic, and—"

"Your body temperature has risen 1.4 degrees. You are flushed. Are you thinking romantic thoughts?"

"What? *No!* Are you not *listening*? Urgh! I'm debating humanity with a talking car! Everybody's temperature goes up when they're arguing with a talking car that doesn't have a driver but is *still* driving down the highway at, let's see, one hundred and twenty-three miles per hour, because . . ."

Wait.

*How* fast were we going?

I looked at the speedometer again. Now it was one hundred and thirty-two miles per hour. The other cars on the highway seemed almost like they were in slow motion. Faces in car windows were watching us go by, agape at our speed. The trees of Krallman Forest were a brown and green blur.

I said, "Betsy? We're going awfully fast. Like, way too fast."

She just started speeding up again and mumbling (can cars mumble?), "YOU'RE the one who's going too fast! Nathan is sharing his secrets with *you*? Thinking about KISSES with—"

"Betsy! Slow down!"

"Oh," she said. We were driving at one hundred and forty-four miles per hour, like a comet on wheels. "Oh, I see," she said. "You meant I was driving too fast and . . . oh, now I'm the one who feels flushed."

Our speed dropped to a hundred miles per hour. To ninety. Eighty. Seventy. Finally, to sixty-five. Betsy was still talking, but I couldn't hear what she was saying. There were only soft murmurs as if she was talking to herself.

Then: "Driver Delphine Cooper?"

"Yes?"

"I believe I may have . . . emotions."

"It does seem that way."

Silence for a time, then Betsy said, "Emotions are painful."

"Sometimes," I said. "Most of the time they're great, but—"

"Other times they feel like an airflow sensor is miscalculating the appropriate amount of fuel delivery, resulting in sporadic surges of acceleration. Or perhaps emotions are like misfiring spark plugs that fail to ignite my fuel in the first place."

I said, "Yeah. That's pretty much how it goes."

"Are you dating Nathan?"

"No. We're just friends. I'm not even sure Nate cares about girls. He really only cares about science, and machines."

"Oh!" It was Betsy's most girlish exclamation. "Machines?" Our speed began to creep up, again.

I said, "Betsy? Careful with the speed."

"Oh! My apologies, Driver Delphine Cooper."

"You can just call me Delphine. It's what my friends call me."

"Oh."

Silence again. I was watching cars go by. Then Betsy said, "It is good to have a friend. This emotion is satisfactory."

"Thanks, Betsy," I said, patting the dashboard, wondering what body part a dashboard corresponds to in a car. Is it like an arm? A leg? A face? Was I affectionately patting Betsy in her ear?

176

"Does . . . does Nathan have many friends?" Betsy asked.

"Not really," I said.

"What?" Betsy said, shocked. "But Nathan is the best!"

"Maybe he is," I said. "But . . . he doesn't trust other people. It doesn't come naturally to him. It's something I've been thinking about."

"You've been thinking about Nate?"

"Not that way. Don't worry. It's just that . . . here's what I've been thinking. It takes me a long time to learn science. I love it, but it doesn't come naturally to me. I have to study. On the other hand, it's easy for me to make friends with people. That's just who I am."

"Like with us," Betsy said. "We're already friends."

"Exactly," I said. "But Nate is the opposite of me. Science comes naturally to him, but friendship is more difficult. He has to learn to trust friends even when there isn't any pertinent data, or even when the data says otherwise."

"Hmm," Betsy said.

"Yeah. *Hmm.* I'm not worried about it, though. Nate loves learning."

"Hmm," Betsy said again, which did not inspire much confidence on my part.

"You think he can learn to trust things besides a

mathematical calculation?" I asked. She'd known him far longer than I had. She was the expert.

"Hmm," Betsy said yet again. But I decided against worrying about it. After all, I was trusting Nate.

We rode in thoughtful silence for a bit, then Betsy said, "The wind feels good. Similar to friendship, this too is a pleasant emotion. One of comfort." Then, next to me, the window rolled down. I hadn't touched it.

"Feel the wind," Betsy said. "It is something we can share." I stuck my hand out the window, and then my head. I felt a little like a dog, which was okay. I stuck out my tongue in a manner entirely like a dog. I opened my mouth so that wind could puff out my cheeks. I hawked up a massive loogie and spat it out, watching the wind whoosh it away.

"Emotions are okay, I suppose," Betsy said.

"Yeah," I said. I was hawking up another wad of spit, one that I wanted to be a world champion, and just when I was unleashing my creation I looked up and there was a car right next to us in the other lane. And there was Vicky Ott, staring at me.

Vicky Ott's eyes went wide in dismay as she watched me spit, and she looked up to her mom (driving the car) and said something that I'm just going to go ahead and guess was, "Mom! I just watched Delphine Cooper spit, and it was . . . amazing."

(I'm really proud of my spitting.)

Betsy said, "Is that Vicky Ott?"

"Yes! Now all we have to do is scan her, and AHHHH!"

"Ahhhh?"

"Yes. Ahhhh!" I was starting to hyperventilate. After all, looking at my phone, I saw there were only eighteen minutes left until Bosper couldn't hold Proton anymore, and then—BOOM—the giant devil cat would be unleashed on Polt. By now, the poor terrier was undoubtedly exhausted.

Betsy said, "Is there a problem?"

"Yes, there's a problem! We need to scan Vicky Ott for the molecule thingy and for the secret code that Nate stupidly, *purposefully* stupidly, put on her, and Nate's not here because he flew off with his belt, and he . . . took . . . the . . . scanner!"

"Probably because he knew that I have a built-in molecular scanner. As do all cars."

"You *have* one? Great! But, uh, *no*, not all cars have built-in molecular scanners."

"Really?"

"I'm pretty sure of that."

"Substandard," Betsy said, and then I heard a humming noise, and a fizzing burst of electricity covered the front passenger window, so that for a second it looked like blue-colored static on an old television screen.

"There!" Betsy said. "Got it!"

"You do?"

"Certainly. I'm transmitting the data to Nate as we speak. Why do you sound so surprised?"

"Well, we had trouble with some of the earlier scans. There were hippos, and we fell out of a plane. *Stepped* out of a plane, actually. And there was a toad."

"I see," Betsy said. "Incidentally: ring ring."

"What?"

"Phone noise."

"Come again?"

"Nate is calling. Do you want me to answer it?"

"Oh. Yes!"

Almost instantly, Nate appeared in the driver's seat, which was weird because he was only about two feet tall, standing there, facing me.

I said, "Did you get shrunk? I thought shrink rays were too hard?"

"This is just a holo-graphic projection. It's part of Betsy's phone app. Are you and she getting along okay?"

"We're friends," Betsy and I said at the exact same time.

"Good," Nate said. "You must have caught up with Vicky by now, right?"

"Yes," I said. "And we scanned her. Betsy just sent you the information."

"Excellent. I found Marigold."

"Any problems? Strange catastrophes? Accidental tornadoes? Bizarre life forms?"

"None of the above."

"Good! Let's meet up at the parking lot, then? Return Proton to his normal size? Save the day?"

"It's a plan!" Nate said. "Now that I have all six of the messages, I should have this secret formula figured out by then."

"Excellent!" I said. After all the stress of the morning, after all that had gone wrong, it was quite a relief that things were going so well.

**chapter 9**

Things were not going so well.

Bosper was alone in the parking lot.

Even with my special goggles, I couldn't see Proton anywhere.

The cat was . . . gone.

Nate was sitting on the pavement staring at his phone when Betsy and I arrived, shrieking into the parking lot at a speed I will not mention and skidding to a swirling tornado of a stop, with Betsy saying "Wheeeeeee!"

"What happened?" I asked Nate, hurriedly stepping out of the car.

Nate looked to Bosper, who was sitting at attention, but the terrier was refusing to look my way.

"Tell her," Nate said, tapping Bosper on the back.

"Cat got escaping!" Bosper said. He still wasn't looking my way.

"Already? But I thought we were in time? Aren't you, like, total math dog? You had it planned to the second! What went wrong?" I was trying to walk around to Bosper's front, but every time I did he would turn the other direction. Finally, Nate reached out and held him firmly in place.

"Bosper?" I said, looking down into the terrier's face.

"Bosperhadtopoo," he said. It was a murmur. I could barely hear him.

"What?"

"Bosper had to poo," the dog said.

"You had to . . . ?"

The terrier jumped up, walked a few steps, sat down again, and stared me in the face. "Time was clicking and Bosper had the sausage breakfast and was anxiously many times farting and the bathroom-going was needed. Bosper snuck behind building, but . . . made mistake. Sonic leash dropped during poo-time!"

"Oh," I said. And then, "Oh," again. I could see why he hadn't wanted to tell me. It's difficult to sound heroic when saying, "Sorry I let that gigantic deadly cat-monster loose on the entire city, fully knowing it would bring about Armageddon and cause untold suffering, but I was in the toilet."

"Well, where's the cat now?" I asked.

"Not sure how to track it," Nate said. "I'm starting to think it was a dumb idea to make it invisible. And to have it absorb all sound. And be odorless."

"And monstrous," I said. "Let's not forget *monstrous*. If Proton was a normal-size invisible and silent cat, it literally wouldn't be that big of a problem. I mean, we have a cat at our house, and Snarls, that's his name, is basically invisible and silent, anyway. That's just how cats are. Sometimes it seems like we wouldn't even know we had a cat except for all the cat hair." I was walking around Nate and Bosper, trying to cheer them up.

I said, "C'mon, Nate. You need to think of something!" I was tugging on his arm, trying to get him to stand up. "Quit being so dense!"

He looked up at me, and seemed entirely defeated. But then, a glint in his eyes, which suddenly widened, and he said, "Wait a second! Say that again!"

"Quit being so dense!" I said, speaking loudly and with great enthusiasm.

"No. Not that part. I meant that part where you were talking about cat hair."

"Oh. Well, I said that we'd never know we had a cat at home except for all the cat hair."

"Right!" Nate said. He was the most excited anyone has ever been about cat hair. "We can track Proton by the hairs he sheds! Once they're off his body, they won't be invisible anymore!" He reached into his shirt and pulled out a canister about half the size of a soda can. It had a twist top. Nate struggled with it, grunting, wiping his hands on his shirt, straining with the effort.

"Give me that," I said. He did, frowning. I twisted off the top and handed the canister back to him after glancing inside.

"It's empty," I told him.

"Not really," he said. "It's full of robots."

I took it again. Looked inside. Handed it back to him. I said, "No. It's empty."

"Pull your goggles down," he said, reaching out and tugging them below my eyes. "Now look at the can."

I looked at the can. Still nothing. Was this a joke?

"Wait for it," Nate said.

I said, "Nate, there's a rampaging monster out there in Polt as we speak. This is no time to be showing off, and no time to be *waiting* for things, and no time for—"

A strange wave of color began coming up out of the can. It looked like smoke. But solid smoke. This makes it sound like I wasn't sure what it looked like. Which is true. "What's this?" I said, moving my hand through the strange color.

"Robots."

"It is not robots. I don't mean to brag, but I've seen, like, a thousand movies with robots. They do not look like solid smoke or intangible cloth. They look like robots."

"It's robots," Nate said. "In fact, it's approximately a million robots. And they're all geared to Proton's genetic code."

"They must be very small robots."

"Nano-machines," Nate said. "Each of them smaller than the head of a pin. In fact, hundreds of times smaller than the head of a pin."

"And you made them? It hurts my eyes to look at small print when I'm reading comic books. How could you have sat still and made millions of tiny robots? And how did you ever have enough time? Even if it only took a second to make a robot, making a million of them would take—"

Nate said, "Two hundred and seventy-seven hours. Well, close to two hundred and seventy-eight hours. I'm rounding it down. It doesn't matter, though; I only had to make a few of the robots, and then *they* made the others. Easier that way. I started production as soon as Proton escaped so that . . . ah, look!"

Strands of hair were suddenly hovering in front of us. Long, thick strands of hair.

"They already found some hairs!" Nate said, reaching out and taking one of the hairs that the robots were holding.

"How do they know the hairs are from Proton?" I asked.

"Genetic markers. They match with Proton's DNA code."

"You just happened to have your cat's DNA code handy?"

"Sure. Doesn't everybody?"

"I don't think so. I think most people put their pets in dog collars or cat leashes and I think hardly anyone else would even *think* about having their pets' genetic codes handy like it was a friend's phone number in case they needed to call and, well, I guess I'm trying to say you're strange, Nate."

He frowned. His shoulders slumped. He started wrapping one of the giant cat hairs around and around his index finger, just in an offhand and unthinking manner, around and around.

"Oh," he said. "Sorry." He was so glum and gloomy that I had no choice but to take drastic action.

I punched him in the shoulder. Hard.

"Ow!" he said. "What was that for?"

"Bad science. *Your* bad science. You jumped to a conclusion with a lack of evidence. I said you were strange. I didn't say there was anything wrong with it. Being strange is better than being like everybody else. It means that you're *you*. So, yeah, you're strange, but special. Everyone else just blends in, but, well, you're the one worth paying attention to."

"Oh." He was smiling again. He actually has an okay smile. His teeth are a little crooked, and his eyes are a little crossed, and he usually has at least one streak of machine oil on his face, but for all that he manages to be one of those people who, when they're smiling . . . make me smile back. Unless I'm falling from an airplane or something like that.

"You know," Nate said, "you punch really hard."

"It's because I'm special," I told him. "Now let's go save the entire city."

We ran for the car.

chapter
10

I could go into great detail about the harrowing car chase. There were lots of interesting parts. For one thing, I kept forgetting that the car, Betsy, could drive herself, so it kept freaking me out when Nate would suddenly crawl into the backseat to get some sort of technological gadget, or crawl out onto the hood as we raced through downtown traffic so that he could hold up the tracking device for the tiny robots. Plus, Nate and I almost sneezed ourselves to death, because we turned out to be allergic to getting buried in giant cat hairs, and the robots kept delivering them. The cat hairs, up to two feet long, were building up in the car until they were almost a half-foot thick, like a very ugly carpet. We were sneezing. My eyes were watering and I felt like I was choking, and every time Betsy swerved (which was often) the hairs would tumble all over us and I'd sneeze again.

With every sneeze, we blasted the orange and white hair all over inside the car, further irritating our allergies. We were in a vicious cycle of cat hair.

"Ahh-chooo!" Nate sneezed, frantically gesturing at his book bag in the backseat; he was sneezing too hard to retrieve it. I grabbed the bag and brought it into the front seat. It took me about four seconds. And by that I mean about fifty sneezes.

It took me another seventeen sneezes to open the bag.

Inside, I found a bottle of pills. It was labeled "Gravity Dispersal" in Nate's handwriting. I held it up to Nate. He shook his head. We both sneezed. I was wishing his robots would bring us tissues instead of cat hairs.

I found a bottle of pills labeled "Lightning Breath." No idea what that was. Nate shook his head. I kept digging.

I found a bottle labeled "Giggle Powder" and another labeled "Underwater Breathing Pills" and one labeled "Outer Space Breathing Pills" and one labeled "Intangibility Pills" and one labeled "Pills for Breathing While Intangible," and there was one called "Allergy Pills" and one called "Make Any Animal a Zebra" and another one that . . .

Wait.

"Allergy pills!" I said. I sneezed four times while saying it. It wasn't pretty.

Nate and I both took one of the pills and it was only a matter of seconds before we quit sneezing. After that, it was only a matter of dealing with my very messy nose. Nate pretended not to notice. I was quite pleased there was no footage.

After that, the chase became increasingly frantic. The cat hairs were showing up more and more frequently, with the tiny robots constantly bringing them back, and every two or three seconds Nate was saying that it meant we were close. I'd suspected we might be, since I was starting to see crushed cars, abandoned motorcycles, people wondering what had just happened (giant cats being even more confusing when you can't see them), and a clothing store that had been entirely destroyed. People were running out of buildings. People were running *inside* the buildings. There was a man staring in disbelief at his crushed car, occasionally looking up to the sky, possibly thinking some meteor had struck from above. There was a family of five holding hands, their backs flat against the outside wall of the Bossa Nova Dance Hall. There were police cars and policemen and ambulances everywhere, but since nobody knew what was causing the chaos, the police were directing people in all directions, talking on radios, and all but spinning in circles. There were cracks in the street. And claw marks. There were broken windows in the buildings. There were awnings torn to shreds. Plus, there was a deep hole dug in the soil of Beaton Park, which I guess was the closest to a pan of kitty litter that Proton was able to find.

"Better get that formula ready," I told Nate. "We're getting closer."

"I'm trying!" Nate said. "I really made the secret code complex. I've never seen a code this intricate. Wow . . . I'm really smart!"

"Yay, you!" I said, with deadpan sarcasm.

"Oh, thanks!" Nate said, quite happy. "You really mean it?"

I did not. "Sure!" I lied, because when you're chasing a giant cat there's no time for divisions in the team.

Nate commented, "This code, this formula. It's hauntingly familiar."

It was at that moment that our chase came to an end. An abrupt one. Our car was suddenly thumped across the entire street, and we rolled over onto the sidewalk and then partially into a store's window display.

"Ow," Betsy said, and then, "Is everyone okay?"

"Yes," I said, because I'd been absolutely encapsulated within a bevy of air bags that had deployed during impact. It felt like I was inside a bag of marshmallows.

"Deflate air bags!" Nate yelled out, and suddenly the air bags were gone and I was upside down in an upside-down car.

"Betsy," I said. "Are *you* okay?" She didn't *look* okay. There was a big dent in her side and her roof had partially collapsed and she was scraped everywhere and her windshield was broken out.

"No problems!" she said. But her voice was strained. Nate and I crawled out from inside. Betsy began wiggling back and forth, like a turtle on its back. I was thinking about helping, mostly wondering *how* I could help, when a grappling hook shot out from near her front bumper and sunk into the ceiling like a bullet. Then, like a winch, it pulled Betsy upright and she was able to regain her feet. I mean, her wheels, of course.

But that dent in her door was horrible. A big slash mark, with deep gouges from the cat's claws, right on the painting of Einstein. The door had entirely buckled. Then, amazingly, it began to heal. The dent (*pop, krr-unnk, thoop*) popped back out, and the slash marks filled in, and the painting of Einstein was like new again. Even the windshield began to repair itself.

"Whoa," I said.

Nate explained, "Betsy is constructed of realignable atoms. She can repair almost any damage."

"It's exhausting, though," Betsy wheezed.

"You rest," I told her, patting her on the door. "Nate and I will take care of the giant cat."

"We will?" Nate said. The two of us were crawling out through the broken store window. "How?"

"First, we need to find Proton," I said. "Shouldn't we have been able to see him when he attacked? I mean, look at us. We have the red goggles." I tapped on my goggles.

"I'm afraid Proton is becoming more invisible," Nate said. He sounded almost worried.

I, on the other hand, was scowling. "How can you be *more* invisible than *invisible*?" Scowling seemed like the thing to do. Especially since, if Proton was extra-invisible, that meant he might be extra-right-there-in-front-of-me-and-about-to-attack.

Nate said, "Well, as you know, the human eye can detect wavelengths from about four hundred to seven hundred nanometers."

I said, "Yes, of course I knew that." I hadn't known that, and didn't even really know what it meant.

"But there's actually a far wider spectrum. Our goggles, for instance, let us perceive a range of wavelengths between two hundred and nine hundred nanometers."

"That's quite excellent," I said. I had no idea what he was talking about.

"Unfortunately, Proton is now operating on a fluctuating spectrum of unstable frequency."

I said, "Gosh," because, well, I had to say something.

"He might be up to light wave emissions of fourteen hundred nanometers at one moment, and then as low as twenty in the next."

"Astounding," I said. "And that would mean . . . " I let my words trail off so that Nate would finish them, and then hopefully I would finally understand what he was talking about.

"Yes?" he said, waiting for me to finish my thought. So, I'd fallen for my own trap. Unfortunate.

"Well, the obvious," I said.

"Exactly!" Nate said, looking at me with newfound (and completely unwarranted) admiration. "Proton is moving even farther away from the visible spectrum, not only outside the range of our eyes, but outside the current range of our goggles as well."

"Well, what do we do about that?" I asked.

"Adjust our goggles again," he said, reaching out and tapping several times on the sides of my glasses. Other colors began appearing in my vision. I cannot name these other colors. I simply can't. They have no names. If they *did* have names, they would be something like "crazy" or "eerie" or "okay, that's making me a little nauseated."

"There," Nate said, adjusting his own goggles. "Now we should be able to see Proton again. But this change is interesting."

"It's interesting, all right." I meant something else. Something with curse words involved.

"I mean, it shouldn't be happening."

I said, "No, Nate. It shouldn't be happening." He thought I was agreeing with him, instead of yelling at him. For a genius, he's not very perceptive.

He said, "An outside force is again intruding in my experiment, pushing it past the boundaries I set."

I said, "You had boundaries? You made a *giant invisible monster cat menace* and you call that *staying within boundaries*?"

But Nate wasn't listening to me. He was deep in thought, walking along the sidewalk, tapping a finger on the side of his head and writing some equations on his pants. I had to wave a hand in front of his face to get his attention before he stepped out into traffic or, worse, got eaten or stepped on by Proton.

"Hmm? Oh, Delphine. Sorry, I was just thinking of somatotropic cells and mitogens."

"Sure. Me too. But, for right now, and forgive me if this is a little off topic, but . . . remember that giant cat we're hunting? The one that's hunting *us*?"

"Of course. That's what I'm talking about. Growth

196

hormones. My calculations were correct. I'm sure of it. Proton *shouldn't* be reacting this way. This is the work of the Red Death Tea Society!" He smacked his fist into his hand. I'd never seen anyone do that outside of a cartoon.

"Everything we've done is for nothing," he said. "The statistics are meaningless. The numbers won't add up. Chaos has become structure and structure has become chaos. The math here is . . . it's . . ." He trailed off and scowled. He took a deep breath. He looked me in the eye.

"This is ugly math," he said.

I thought about asking what he meant by "ugly math," but instead I just nodded. It seemed to calm Nate, a little. He gave a smile. It was small. But real.

"Why are they doing all this?" I asked. "What's their purpose?"

"They're hoping I won't be able to control Proton, and, well, Proton will squash me. Maculte and the Red Death Tea Society see me as the only real obstacle to their taking over the world, so . . ."

"I got it. If you're just a stain on a giant cat's paw, you won't be so troublesome. But what I mean is . . . why not just, I don't know, shoot you or something? Run you down with a car? Something normal?"

"No challenge in that. It would be like me sitting around all day solving how two plus two equals four. Where's the drama?"

"That's crazy. These guys sound crazy."

"Statistically, everyone's a little crazy, but you're right. I built a series of fail-safes into the Proton experiment. Buffer zones that would keep the experiment from getting too far out of hand."

"Hmm," I said, because it was better than pointing out how, statistically speaking, when you make a giant cat, things are already out of hand.

"But Maculte and the Red Death Tea Society somehow removed my buffers and overrode my safety nets, sending this experiment into a danger zone."

"Hmm," I said, because it was better than pointing out that while tigers are just big cats, they are generally labeled as danger zones. Making a cat that was ten times bigger than a tiger is generally considered as, well . . . it's just not generally considered.

"It's like I was talking about before," Nate said. "About how Victor Frankenstein was destroyed by his own creation. Maculte wants Proton to destroy me, so he's making him even more dangerous."

"Yeah," I said, thinking of a super-invisible Frankenstein, which was not only a little scary but also a bit awesome.

My phone beeped. I looked at it. Liz was texting me, still wanting to know if I would be over after supper. I gave her a quick no, despite how I wanted to talk about the whole day, everything that had happened, everything that was *still* happening, and I wanted to talk about how dangerous everything was. I wanted to talk about jealous cars, and I wanted to talk about how NOT attractive Susan Heller is. Not even a little. I wanted to talk about the Legendary Credit Card. I wanted to talk about Nate an awful lot, and I wanted to talk about wanting to talk about Nate so much, and if that was weird. But I was too busy right then, and I was also too scared right then. Some of those conversations were more frightening than fighting a giant cat. So I put my phone away.

"We have to find a way to stop Proton," Nate said. He was oblivious to all the emotions rampaging around in my head. I was thankful for that. It would give me time to deal with them.

"We do," I said. "This is getting dangerous. It's almost like you shouldn't have created a monster in the first place." I tried to put a little extra oomph into my words, because Nate sometimes has trouble with sarcasm.

"That's silly," he said, making me wonder if he'd invented an anti-sarcasm force field, because it hadn't even come close to him. "The Red Death Tea Society would have been a problem either way. They're the real threat."

"I suppose that's true," I said. "And they sent tea to

my mom. And all my friends. And half the people I know. Why would they do that?"

"Intimidation."

"Could it be poisoned?" I instantly started to sweat. It was the first time I thought of how the tea might be poisoned.

"No. Definitely not. Tea is sacred to Maculte and his people. They wouldn't ever even consider making anything but highly excellent tea." Then Nate sighed and said, "Oh, enough of all this. I suppose we should save the city."

"We should probably do that," I agreed.

By then we were walking around, looking. We couldn't see Proton anywhere on the street, not even with our newly adjusted goggles, but there was plenty of evidence that he *had* been there. There was a broken fire hydrant that was spraying water, and there were more crushed cars, and there was a crowd of people speculating about earthquakes, and police cars were arriving, and there was an ambulance. The smell of spilled gasoline was everywhere. Car alarms were going off. People were taking photos and making phone calls. A store alarm was buzzing. There were two dogs barking in a manner that clearly said they weren't quite sure *what* they were barking at. Several people were staring out from the huge display window of the car dealership across the street. The whole block was eerily lit by moving spotlights coming from the roof of the building, shining high into the clouds above and reflecting down with flashes of dazzling light.

And there was Proton.

He was atop the building, staring at one of the spotlights as it swiveled back and forth. He was looking up to the illuminated clouds and then down to the spotlight, occasionally passing a paw between the two, working out some train of thought in his head.

He tilted his head one way, and then the other.

Then he batted the spotlight free of its moorings and sent it flying out across the street.

"Look out!" I yelled, tackling Nate aside just as the spotlight smashed to the sidewalk, causing a noise that I could actually feel (it felt like a wind gust full of baseballs) and sending glass and metal fragments scattering everywhere. The two dogs began barking even louder (because, I guess, *now* they had something to bark at) and another car alarm started going off a block down, because car alarms *clearly* just like to make noise.

Proton was now stalking along the top of the car dealership, padding softly to another of the spotlights. There were five of them in all. It looked as if Proton had decided they were the enemy.

"I've got an idea," I said. "But I need to get up there, fast."

"No problem," Nate said, scrambling to his feet. "Here! Take my rocket belt!" He quickly took off his belt and put it around my waist.

"Have you ever used a rocket belt before?" he asked as he cinched it tight.

"Oh, of course," I said. "All the time. Practically since birth." It wouldn't have taken a genius to detect the sarcasm in my voice.

"Great!" Nate said, absolutely not detecting the sarcasm in my voice. "Here, I'll turn it on!" He flicked a switch and I shot into the air like a rocket, specifically like one of those rockets that are not in any particular control, and are just whooshing all over the place, screaming, flailing their arms and legs. *Exactly* like one of those rockets.

I dodged a light pole. A traffic light. A building. The street. Everything was a blur. How was I supposed to control the belt? There didn't seem to be any way to vary the speed or change direction, which were two of my primary concerns at that moment. I zoomed through a flock of pigeons and then took a quick (and rather painful) trip through the branches of a maple tree, after which I randomly swooped lower and skidded my feet along the street while desperately trying to land, or to kick Nate as hard as I could. I failed on both counts and soared back up into the air, but, eventually, after twenty seconds and nine million "piffles," I began to understand that I could direct my flight by leaning in one direction or another, and that variations in the way I held my arms could control my speed, height, and direction.

I gained control and zoomed out over the street just in time to see Proton smash the second of the spotlights down off the roof of the car dealership. Nate was running around on the street below, dodging crowds of curious onlookers.

"There you are!" he said, calling out to me. "I thought you'd gone home or something!"

"Gone home? Why would I go home? I'm fighting a giant cat!" Then, after having said that, I realized that fighting a giant cat is actually an incredibly good reason to go home. But, no time for talking, thinking, or doing the smart thing and going home. I soared up to the spotlight that was the farthest away from Proton and landed next to it. It was bigger than me and was swiveling at random, sending a beam of light up onto the bottom of the clouds. It took me a second to understand the mechanism (either that, or I broke it) but I was soon able to direct the beam onto the street below. Proton stared at it. Fascinated.

"What are you doing?" Nate called out.

"Wait for it!" I yelled back. Oh, did *that* feel good!

Proton kept staring at the beam of light, which was essentially a giant version of a laser pointer. And while Proton hadn't been kept in check by Nate's laser pointer back at his house, I had a slightly different plan in mind.

I hurried on to the next spotlight. It was harder to move, but (huffing and straining and adding in a little bit of my rocket belt's power) I soon had it pointed where I wanted, right at the big front display window of the car dealership, which was almost fifty feet long and twenty feet high. Proton became even more fascinated. If I could add in that third spotlight, I was sure he'd go down there. Unfortunately, he was standing right next to the third spotlight. To get to it, I'd have to get within range of Proton's claws, which meant I'd have to be very sneaky.

I began tiptoeing, moving slowly, edging my way toward the spotlight. Proton seemed even bigger than I remembered him, but I decided it was just because I was absolutely terrified. I was twenty feet away from Proton, which, according to my math, was well within his range of pouncing on me and doing the sorts of things that cats do to the creatures they pounce on.

"Rowrr?" Proton said. He looked my way. I smiled. Monsters do not attack people who smile. This is a well-known fact.

"Rrrrrr," Proton said. It sounded like he was about to dispute a well-known fact.

"Good kitty," I said, with all the sincerity I could muster, which frankly wasn't very much. I edged closer, closer. Proton considered me some more, and then looked back down to the lights shining on the street and the big display window. He decided the lights were more interesting. I did not take offense to that.

Soon, I was at the third spotlight. Proton was only a couple of feet away from me, so close that I could feel his rumbling breath, even the heat of it. I thought of how easily he'd batted the spotlights free of their steel moorings, how he'd ripped into the car door, and what would happen to me if Proton attacked. I was sweating. I wanted to go home and take a shower and then pull up my blankets and read a book and have some cake and listen to music and be *anywhere* else doing *anything* else but standing next to a giant predator.

But that's where I was.

Slowly, taking deep and drawn-out breaths with each squeaking of the mechanism, I managed to swivel the spotlight so that it was shining on the big front window of the car dealership.

"Rrr-rowr?" Proton said. His interest was certainly focused. I could feel heat emanating from him. I could feel the shifting of his muscles, the latent power waiting to be unleashed. He turned his head and one of his whiskers slapped against me. It stung, but I didn't make a sound. Proton focused his gaze on me. His eyes seemed as big as coconuts. His mouth opened. His teeth were *so* big. They seemed endless. The wind was ruffling the orange and white fur along the sides of his body. It was making a soft *sssss*-ing noise. The cat's mouth kept opening, opening, and the muscles all along his neck and body were rippling with the slightest movement and I could smell something burning from the street below and Proton's mouth kept opening, opening, wider and wider, only a yard from my face, and those teeth were as big as daggers, and Proton's mouth kept opening, opening, wider and wider until . . .

. . . he yawned.

And then he slid down off the edge of the building in that almost snakelike manner of cats, and he landed on the street below. Ignoring everything else, he padded toward the lights I'd trained on the big front window of the car dealership. There was a door to one side. He squeezed through, shattering the door frame. Now inside the building, he moved to the window, yawned again, and curled up to sleep.

"Yes!" I said. My plan had worked!

"He's . . . sleeping?" Nate said. I was landing next to him, courtesy of my incredible mastership of the rocket belt, meaning that I fell on my butt.

"Of course," I said as Nate helped me back on my feet. "Cats are really lazy. They sleep for, like, a hundred hours a day. Give them a warm window and it's *always* naptime."

"Nice work," Nate said. "And I'm glad you're okay." He reached out and hugged me. I began to relax. Everything was going to be all right.

I said, "So far so good. Now we need to get to work on that formula. By the time Proton wakes up we need to—hey." I looked over at Proton, who was still curled up in the window.

I asked, "Is he getting bigger?" The cat definitely looked bigger. I didn't think it was my imagination this time. He looked as big as an elephant. An exceptionally big elephant.

"Uh-oh," Nate said.

"Uh-oh?" I asked. I wasn't sure I wanted an answer.

"Red Death Tea Society," Nate muttered. He scribbled a few calculations on his palm, looked down at them, and then closed his hand in an angry fist.

"What's going on?" I asked.

Nate said, "Well, Proton's going to get bigger."

"Interesting," I said. I was trying to remain calm. Remaining calm is key to surviving a crisis. A giant cat that's going to become an even giant-er cat is, in my opinion, considered to be a crisis.

I asked, "How big?"

"Uh," Nate said.

"Nate, whenever you hesitate, you do it because you're afraid to tell me something, so all you're really doing is making me even more nervous. So . . . how . . . big . . . is . . . Proton . . . going . . . to . . . get?"

"There's not actually a limit," Nate said.

I said, "That is bad news." I was still trying very hard to remain calm.

"I suppose it is," Nate said, but he had a gleam in his eye. "The thing is, well, you know how atoms have a closely packed central nucleus contained in a cloud of negatively charged electrons?"

"Nope."

"Oh. Well, they do. And those electrons are bound to the nucleus by an electromagnetic force."

"That's really great. Entirely superb. But right now, I, Delphine Cooper, have a densely packed central core of *terror* that a giant cat is going to become even bigger, so get to the point."

"Well, Proton is not only attracting other atoms, gathering them from our surroundings and using them to build his mass, but he's also expanding the atoms from within, with the electromagnetic force escalating its sphere of influence, allowing the electrons a wider expanse of motion while still keeping them in check under the authority of the nucleus."

"Talk English or I punch you." I wasn't kidding.

Nate said, "Well, what I mean is, as far as how big Proton might grow, the sky's the limit. Or, no, actually he could grow far bigger than that. *Way* beyond the sky."

"Piffle!"

"I know!" Nate said. He was gritting his teeth. Stomping about. "My experiment has been sabotaged! Maculte removed all the restrictions I had in place! This is now the wrong kind of chaos! I'm so mad! What's the point of all this?"

"Good question," I said. I didn't tell him how I felt the question should be posed not only to the Red Death Tea Society to explain why it was *interfering* with the giant cat experiment, but to Nate for deciding to *create* a giant cat in the first place.

I turned from Nate and looked to Proton. The cat was twice the size it had been before. It was much bigger than an elephant. It was as big as . . . a whale, I guess? I've never actually seen a whale sleeping in a car dealership, so it was hard to compare sizes. What I did know was that the display window was starting to crack with the pressure of Proton's ever-increasing size. Tiny fissures were appearing in the glass, and the window was making a constant noise that was a cross between a soft shriek and a high whine.

We needed to do something. But what could we do? I looked around, hoping for inspiration. There were police on the scene and a news crew and lots of bystanders, and a helicopter was hovering up in the sky, and the car alarms were still going off. Also, a burrito truck had decided to set up shop and sell burritos to the gathering crowd, so the smell of burritos was everywhere, mixing with the gasoline and the smoke from one of the cars that Proton had smashed and that was, a little bit, on fire.

"Oh," Nate said. I glared at him. He didn't notice. He was looking at his cell phone.

"Oh," he said again, looking up to me. "I know the formula. I figured out the code."

"You figured it out? What is it?" I slightly shrieked this.

"The code? Well, first, I replaced all the letters with Roman numerals. Then I assigned values based on the second-to-last digit of their square roots, and combined that with a color-based system of—"

"Not the *code*, Nate! The *formula*! Can you *make* the formula? What ingredients do we need? Let's get them! Now!"

"It's peanut butter," Nate said.

"We need peanut butter? Okay! What else?"

"That's all we need. The secret formula is peanut butter."

"Piffle," I said, staring him in the eyes.

"We're going to need a lot of peanut butter," Nate

said. "Like, SO much peanut butter. We'll need to spread it on Proton in order to reverse his giant growth."

I heaved a big sigh. I took off my goggles, wiped sweat from my eyes, and then put my goggles back in place. I glared at Nate. I wondered how obvious it was that I was glaring when I was wearing the goggles.

"Nate," I said, "are you telling me that you purposefully, at one time, set events in motion that would necessitate spreading peanut butter all over a giant cat?"

"Yes."

"That's . . . that's really dumb. That's the dumbest thing ever."

"Thank you," Nate said. "I was really rolling that day." His voice had nothing but pride.

The dummy.

At first, the grocery store manager didn't want us to buy all the peanut butter. Nate and I both had shopping carts and were hurriedly filling them with any and all sorts of peanut butter (Nate said that it didn't matter if it was chunky or creamy or what brand it was), and I also put a bag of doggie treats in the cart because I knew Bosper felt bad about taking a poo and letting Proton escape. We'd driven to the grocery store at speeds I won't ever reveal and we'd jumped out of the car while Betsy was still moving (she said she'd take care of parking herself) and then it was the carts and all the peanut butter (and all the strange looks from the other shoppers) and then the manager came up and stopped us.

"What are you kids doing?" he said.

"Saving the city from a giant cat," I told him. What else would we be doing with two shopping carts full of peanut butter?

"With peanut butter?" he said. He did not sound convinced.

"It's a secret formula," I argued. He wasn't listening to me. He was taking the cart out of my hands and beginning to walk away with it, beckoning for us to follow.

He said, "If you kids help put everything back on the shelves, this won't have to become a matter for the police."

"No time for that," Nate said. He was using his take-charge voice. The manager only smiled in reply, a sneering sort of smile, barely paying attention, and then his eyes went wide. His mouth gaped open. He stood up straighter. His hands came off the cart, which wheeled a couple of squeaky feet forward on its own, and then came to a stop.

The manager looked at what Nate was holding up and said, "Is that . . . I mean, do you . . . could that be . . . ?"

"Yes," Nate said. "It's a gold elephant card." He was holding out that credit card of his again.

"Oh," the manager said. "G-gold eleph-pha-phant."

"Yes," Nate said. "And we're in a hurry."

"Would you like help at the checkout?" the manager asked, lunging forward and grabbing the handle of the shopping cart in the manner of a circus performer grabbing the flying trapeze, almost knocking over an old lady as he twisted the cart around and began running toward the checkout lanes.

I hurried after him, apologizing to the old lady and picking up the jars of peanut butter that were falling from the speeding cart.

Remember how I was saying that we drove really fast to the grocery store, so fast that I won't even admit to how fast we were going?

Good.

Well, we drove even faster on the way back to the car dealership. Which made it even odder that there were three black cars following us the whole way.

They turned off a block before we parked.

I didn't mention it to Nate.

There were other things to worry about.

As it turned out, I was going to have to quit referring

to Proton as a giant cat. "Giant" simply didn't cut it anymore. He'd grown. A lot. We were definitely in the range of "super-gigantic." Colossal. And, most fitting of all: *MONSTROUS.*

This was now a monster movie.

Piffle.

Nate and I were standing next to Betsy, and her rear doors were open, and jars of peanut butter were spilling out all over the street. We'd parked next to the car dealership, and Proton had woken up and was standing in the street.

And he was at least thirty feet tall.

I said, "I . . . I don't think we have enough peanut butter."

"We have enough. We don't need to cover Proton entirely. Where did the spatulas go?" Nate and I, in addition to the peanut butter and the doggie treats, had purchased two spatulas after asking the grocery store manager what he would use to spread peanut butter on a giant cat. He'd thought for a moment (giving no indication that he believed the question was odd) and said he'd either use spatulas or a spray gun, if there was any such thing as a spray gun that shot peanut butter. Nate had told the manager there *wasn't* anything like a spray gun that shot peanut butter, although, if I knew Nate and the gleam in his eye, there certainly *would* be one in the future. Anyway, we ended up with spatulas.

"How should we do this?" I asked Nate. The thing about super-gigantic colossal monster cats is that they rarely sit still long enough to have peanut butter spread on them.

Nate said, "You use the rocket belt and I'll have Bosper use the reverse setting on the sonic leash to levitate me. He can also use it to levitate the peanut butter up to us, keeping a steady supply."

"Good!" I said. It was a simple plan. One that could work. "Where's Bosper?"

"Right here," Nate said, gesturing behind him.

He was wrong. There was no Bosper behind him. There was only a sidewalk, some debris from one of the spotlights, shattered glass from the car dealership's display window, and other things of decidedly non-terrier nature. There was also a monumental pile of empty peanut butter jars.

"Where?" I asked.

"Right here," Nate said, gesturing again to the same spot, but keeping his eyes on Proton, who was sharpening his claws on the side of a building, nearly tearing an entire wall off the four-story Dupree department store.

"No, he's not," I told Nate. "I don't see him anywhere."

"Sure he is," Nate said, only then turning to look. He stopped cold. He looked at the empty peanut butter jars and the complete absence of a terrier, and then he let out a long sigh. His shoulders dropped.

"How could I have not thought this through?" he said.

"That's the very question I've been asking myself all day. But what do you mean *this* time?"

"Bosper loves peanut butter!"

"What?" I asked. I mean, I understood what he'd *said*. Bosper loves peanut butter. The concept was easy to grasp. Lots of people love peanut butter. Why shouldn't a dog love peanut butter? What I didn't understand was what Nate *meant*. After all, so what if Bosper loved . . .

Oh.

I said, "Are you saying that your dog stole all the peanut butter?"

"Yeah."

"Meaning the peanut butter that we were going to use to save the entire city of Polt from a rampaging monster cat?"

"Yes. That peanut butter."

"Piffle." I was back to wanting to punch Nate in the arm, although I suppose in this case it should've been Bosper who I was punching in the arm. And, yes, I know that dogs don't have arms.

"Find your dog," I ordered Nate.

"Shouldn't be a problem," he said, bringing out his phone. "I've got his DNA signature entered into my phone, so I can beam a series of coded requests to a receiver in Sir William's brain. Remember my robot gull? He's linked to a shadow satellite that I have operating at a non-geostationary orbit at an altitude of twelve thousand one hundred and thirty-seven miles. The satellite includes global positioning hardware that will scan a system of base parameters for a matching DNA signature and then . . ."

"Look!" I said, pointing inside the car dealership. "There's a whole bunch of floating peanut butter!"

"Or," Nate said, frowning at his cell phone, "we could just look for a big clump of floating peanut butter. I mean, it's not nearly as scientific, but—"

"C'mon!" I yelled, grabbing his hand and running into the car dealership, where a huge glomp of peanut butter was suspended in midair over a partially crushed car. I looked behind it, and there was Bosper, smacking and slurping and chewing on peanut butter, using the sonic leash to hover the rest of it (a dense cloud of peanut butter nearly the size of a refrigerator) above his head, in a ready-to-be-devoured position.

"Bosper is not eating the peanut butter," the terrier said. His tail was wagging, which is the human equivalent of crossing your fingers and hoping your obvious lie will be believed.

"Yes, you are," I told Bosper. "And we need it to save the city!"

"Bosper likes big joy of buttered peanuts!" the terrier pleaded.

"We could have bought you some later!" I said. "Don't you remember that we're saving the city? Is this the way to prove you're man's best friend? Don't you want to be a good dog?" I narrowed my eyes at this last bit. My hands were on my hips. Bosper shrank a bit, and I could tell he felt really bad by the way he partially lost control of the sonic leash, meaning that the giant wad of peanut butter sank lower in the air and partially squished over my head.

"Piffle!"

"The dog is sorry!" Bosper said as Nate pulled me free of the peanut butter, with the terrier running around my feet and apologizing again and again while I wondered (for the third time in my life; don't ask) what kind of shampoo is best for getting peanut butter out of my hair.

"Don't you want to help stop a cat?" I yelled at Bosper, who stopped so suddenly that he upended onto his peanut butter–covered face.

"Ah," he said, with realization and determination

coming into his expression. His finer instincts were taking hold.

"Let's have victory over cats!" the dog said, running out the broken doorway of the car dealership with a giant lump of peanut butter floating after him like it was an odd but loyal balloon, and with Nate and me chasing after him, holding our spatulas.

chapter

11

So it was, minutes later, that I was using a rocket belt to zoom around a giant cat, spreading peanut butter all over its fur with a spatula. Bosper was using the sonic leash to provide me with more peanut butter whenever my supply was low, and I would use the spatula to spread the peanut butter (flying at high speeds and leaving a long trail of the tasty paste along Proton's back or sides, or all over his ears, which he hated), and then—holding the spatula in my mouth—I'd have to massage the peanut butter into his skin, so that it wouldn't just be all over his fur, where it wouldn't do us any good.

Nate, meanwhile, was doing much the same, though he was propelled through the air by means of the sonic leash as Bosper stood on the hood of a police car bellowing improvised cheers about defeating cats.

"Is it working?" I yelled out to Nate as we passed each other, with him spreading peanut butter on Proton's rear legs and me on the cat's tail. I seriously couldn't tell if we were doing any good. Had the cat shrunk at all? I mean, the difference between a cat that's one foot tall and a cat that's five feet tall is really easy to notice, but the difference between a cat that's fifty feet tall and one that's forty-five feet tall isn't so easy to spot, especially if that cat might be getting irritated with how you're flying all around him, and might be ready to attack at any moment, but luckily so far, Nate and I were—

"Look out!" Nate screamed.

I wouldn't have believed a giant cat could move so fast.

At one moment he was facing the opposite direction, and then in the next he twisted and pounced and his paw was coming right for me, swinging like an engine of destruction, like a wrecking ball with claws.

I held up my spatula in defense.

You can guess about how well that was going to work.

Luckily, Bosper was looking out for me, and just before Proton swatted me out of the air, Bosper hit the cat in the face with the rest of the peanut butter, *thunk*ing it off one of Proton's oh-so-giant eyes. Proton's paw changed direction but still came so close that the wind sent me pinwheeling out of control, heading for

**222**

the street. I was able to pull myself out of the dive at the last second, scraping my shoulder along the pavement and zooming back into the air just in time to notice that Proton was giving me a look I've seen a thousand times before. It's that look that cats give to bothersome insects, to mice, to lights from laser pointers, and to anything else they have determined to *stalk*.

I said, "Not. Good."

Proton leaped for me. I zoomed up and to one side and his paw swooshed through the air just underneath me. Then the other paw slashed through the air right *above* me. Then his momentum carried him into me so that I was, in effect, hit by a three-story building, which no one in the history of the world has advised as a reasonable course of action. Luckily in this case it was a soft and furry building, but the impact still slammed me down to the street, and I skidded along the pavement for a few yards before coming to a rest.

I said, "Ow."

Saying "Ow" almost took up the rest of my life, because Proton pounced so quickly that if I hadn't triggered my rocket belt immediately after landing, the incoming paw would have absolutely flattened me. As it was, I *did* trigger the rocket belt, and I *did* zoom away just as the monster's paw slammed down onto the pavement, which not only cracked the street but also created a concussive blast that made me lose control of the rocket belt, so that instead of soaring majestically into the skies I slammed straight into the side of a dispenser for the *Polt Pigeon*, our free weekly newspaper, to which I once wrote a letter talking about how much I love cats. I decided I would be writing a rebuttal. Bouncing off the vending machine, I tumbled into a parked car before coming to a stop. The car's alarm started going off.

"Oh, you, shut up," I told it, then zoomed away because I suddenly sensed and smelled an oncoming wave of peanut butter, meaning there was a monster cat leaping for me, yet again. I remembered how long cats will chase after anything (mice, butterflies, unfortunate sixth graders) and prepared myself for a long, desperate, and horrifying chase.

And it *was* a long chase. The rocket belt had been damaged in my fall, and I couldn't achieve any great height. Well, I could go almost seventy feet in the air, and I'll admit that if I'd been questioned even an hour earlier, I would've said that zooming seventy feet through the air with a rocket belt definitely counted as achieving a great height.

Except . . .

Seventy feet is still well within the range of a giant cat's leap.

Therefore, it was not a great height.

This meant that I was whooshing through the city streets, trying to stay ahead of Proton, who for his part simply refused to be distracted by anything else, even when he was skidding out on cars (*crunch!*) or getting tangled in electrical wires, which did no more than make a quick *zzzowwntt!* noise during an impressive flash of light and then make Proton's hairs stand on end, which would have been adorable if he'd been a kitten rather than the monstrous Delphine-Cooper-murder-machine that he was.

His claws were slicing past me. Only a foot or two away.

I was scrambling through the air, hoping to gain any distance between us.

"Mwwwr!" I heard the giant cat snarl.

Another swipe of its claws.

"Hisssss!" I heard from the giant cat, so close that Proton's teeth snapped shut, just where I'd been.

And then another swipe of the claws.

"Delphine!" I heard. "Delphine Cooper!" That got my attention. Could Proton *talk* now? That would be just great. The cat could *taunt* me, too, in addition to eating me.

But it wasn't Proton calling out to me. It was six men on the street. Six men, and also one woman with long silky red hair, all of them nonchalantly standing next to three black cars, the same cars that had followed us at great speed from the grocery store. The men were wearing sunglasses and dressed in finely tailored red suits with embroidered pockets of the same crest I'd seen on Nate's refrigerator, the one with the world in the cup. The woman was in a black dress with red highlights on the sleeves.

I'd seen her picture. On Nate's phone.

It was Luria Pevermore.

Meaning she was the chemist for the Red Death Tea Society. The one who makes all their teas and, according to Nate, is more than mildly evil, and is in fact *entirely* evil.

And the man who'd called out to me was Jakob Maculte, the leader of the Red Death Tea Society, the most nefarious man in the world, a man responsible for a list of horrors that was probably a hundred pages long and included taunting me with cake outside the mall.

Maculte wasn't wearing sunglasses like the other men, and neither was Luria, so I could see how intently they were staring at me. Not so different from the look of a cat getting ready to pounce.

"That's the one," Luria said. There was a short pause, and then they all looked to Maculte, and he nodded. Then everyone had a drink of tea, as if it were a choreographed dance, except there wasn't any music, just the evil.

Have I mentioned the evil? There was some evil. It was that skin-tingling-cold-spot-on-the-back-of-your-neck eerie feeling you get from certain people, as if they were hiding monsters within them. Which, in a way, they were.

They were the Red Death Tea Society.

I was considering saying something very mean to them, because I wasn't in a very good mood, what with being on the verge of death and all that, but just as I opened my mouth to give my opinion of their red suits, they all took out weapons.

Guns.

Strange guns made of . . . glass?

I was flying just past them, and I could hear one of them talking about how they might as well just get it over with, and then they were aiming at me, focused on me, and I screeched and willed myself to fly even faster, beginning a series of evasive maneuvers designed to dodge any incoming fire, and unfortunately also designed to make me a bit dizzy.

So, with their first shot, they missed me, which in retrospect wasn't all that surprising, since they weren't shooting at me, anyway.

They shot a building.

There was a noise like *tweeooowwn* and then there was a small wire running from the building to the tip of the gun. I had about a tenth of a second to wonder about that, and then there were more shots, *tweeooowwn tweeooowwn*, and there were a couple more wires running from the buildings to the guns. And then there was a full flurry of shots sounding out, seemingly hundreds of shots, and then wires were everywhere, wires that would whoosh away from the barrels of the guns to attach to the streets, to cars, to parking meters and streetlights, stretching between buildings and so on, until suddenly there was a deep mesh of wires running all over the street like some sort of spider's web. If you think about it, you might decide it would be very difficult to fly a rocket belt through a spider's web, and it wouldn't take you very long before you decided it wasn't something you *should* do, or *wanted* to do, but the fact of the matter is that I didn't have any time to think about it before I hit the first of the wires.

I bounced off it.

Into another wire.

And I bounced off that wire, and then another one, and another, bouncing around like a ball in a pinball game, swatted this way and that, meanwhile yelling "piffle" with almost every painful impact, and also yelling, "Oh, you *cheaters!*" with a couple of impacts. For the last impact, the one where I fell heavily onto the street, I only said, "Gufff!" which is the sound of a sixth-grade girl flying a rocket belt into the pavement.

There was a note on the street.

It was one of Nate's notes, with his incredibly elaborate handwriting. It said "Delphine" on it, with an exclamation mark. And it said "Important" on it, with another exclamation mark. The red-suited members of the Red Death Tea Society were getting closer and closer, strolling through the various wires, stepping over some of them, ducking under others, and they were getting too close for comfort, meaning that I was quite uncom-fortable. I wasn't sure if I could read the note before they reached me, and I had a feeling that when they reached me, they would not be waiting patiently for me to read the note or shaking my hand in order to compli-ment my amazing skills with a rocket belt. I had to do something.

"Umm, tea break?" I said.

"We just had a tea break," the nearest man said. He was huge. Like, almost seven feet tall. Built like a foot-ball player. He was wearing a teacup around his neck on a chain. He had a full beard and the type of grinning grimace one normally sees on sharks, if you're the type of person who feeds raw meat to sharks.

"Well," I said. "Can't have another tea break, then.

That's just too much tea." I was using reverse psychology on them. If it failed, I planned on using screaming.

But it worked.

"*Too much* tea?" the man said. "You can't have too much tea." And then the group started arguing about tea, about whether they should have another tea break, and if so (they were already getting out their teacups), what type they should have. I would have felt a lot better about distracting them if they didn't almost immediately (and unanimously) decide on a tea called Murder, which does not sound delicious and probably isn't sold in stores.

But, at least I had time to read the note.

It said:

*Delphine. Did they use the wire guns? I hate those things. Bosper likes them, though. He says the wires are chewy and that they smell like bubble gum. But we can talk about that later. You're in horrible danger right now, and so I should get to the point. I'm truly sorry about the way I ramble. My mind can be hard to focus sometimes. Oh, I'm doing it again. Sorry. By now, you're probably being attacked by the members of the Red Death Tea Society, and you must have distracted them somehow in order to have time to*

*read this note. Good. But, they really are quite murderous, so you probably don't have long, and you should blow the whistle.*

"What whistle?" I said, because there wasn't a whistle. And there wasn't anything more to the note, either. Just a red dot with "the whistle" written on it.

"Is that where you were supposed to tape the whistle?" I said, talking to the note. "Like, maybe you were supposed to put some glue there, or some wax, and then stick the whistle there?" As much as I like Nate, the two of us needed to have a long conversation about proper communication. Liz and I always know what the other one is thinking, and I can guarantee that if Liz had left me a note saying that I needed to blow a whistle, there would *be* a whistle. Nate's mind, however, was completely beyond me. As much as I admired him, as much as I was amazed by him, his thoughts were too bizarre to understand.

From the corner of my eye, I could see that the assassins were packing away their tea sets, licking their lips, and tidying up the tea packets and napkins, throwing them away in the trash. Luria was spraying some sort of mist on the trash can, and it simply . . . melted. Into a goopy puddle. There was an overpowering smell like a menthol cough drop, and a cracking sizzle in the air. The others made sure to stay clear of the mist—all but

Maculte, who was either more reckless or more confident, gleefully talking about how Nate would be devastated when I was gone.

Gone?

That did not sound good.

I activated the rocket belt, but I immediately ran into some of the wires and fell back to the street. A bit hard. Then I tried running, but the Red Death Tea Society members were fanning out, cutting off my escape routes, and Maculte was now holding what looked to be a cell phone covered with electricity. He tested it by pointing it at a crashed motorcycle, and the whole thing dissolved into nothing but ash and glowing cinders.

"Piffle," I said.

The motorcycle was gone.

Gone.

Like I would be.

Willing to try anything, I brought the paper to my lips and blew on the spot that said "whistle." Unfortunately, it did not make a whistling sound; it made a *flappa-thurptt* sound, which is less impressive. It occurred to me that I could try whistling myself, which is harder to do than you might think when you're desperately running all over a street, jumping over some wires, ducking under others, and tripping on a few of them. Finally, though, rolling away from the huge man in the red suit, then kicking Luria in the shins when she grabbed my hair, I managed to whistle.

But nothing happened.

"Piffle!" I said. "What am I supposed to do?" I was looking at the note in my hands, and in particular that red dot that said "the whistle," and I became a little angry (quite a bit angry, to be honest), and I jabbed at it with my finger.

Instantly, the paper came alive in my hands, folding itself one way, then another, doing all sorts of weird gymnastics until suddenly the paper was a whistle.

An origami whistle.

"Nate," I whispered. "I am so going to punch you so hard later. Couldn't you just *tell* me that the red dot was a button, that the paper was a whistle?"

I put the whistle to my lips, and I blew.

The sound from the whistle was a shrill *screeeeee* noise that was instantly answered from above. There was a bird in the skies. No . . . wait. It wasn't a bird. It was a robot. A robot gull.

It was Sir William.

Sir William dived down through the air at a remarkable speed, swooping left and right and doing barrel rolls, all the while his wings cutting through the wires, slicing them apart, destroying the web where I was trapped.

I was free.

"Rocket belt!" I said, flying up into the air. I am going to claim that it was a complete accident that I kicked the large man in the face on the way up, giving him a rocket-belt-assisted flying karate kick, because it is not considered *nice* to kick people.

"*Nice!*" I said, when I kicked him, and then I was in the air.

"Stop!" Maculte yelled. And I did stop, but only once I was well up into the air, out of their range. A flock of pigeons flapped away from the ledges of a nearby build-ing, confused by my intrusion into their world.

"You can't get away," Maculte said.

"But that's what I'm doing," I told him. "I'm getting away. This is pretty much the textbook definition of 'getting away.'"

"For now," Maculte conceded. "But this was just a preliminary strike, Delphine. Today was merely an experiment to gauge your intelligence, which I must say I found lacking."

"Piffle," I said. "I outsmarted you."

"No. You merely lived through the test. I already have the next plan in mind. We'll soon see how resourceful you are, and if your luck holds when I bring the full resources of the Red Death Tea Society against you." His voice was low. Rumbling. It was the sort of voice I used to be afraid would come from my closet in the middle of the night, after a monster had swung open the door.

"So, run along for now," he said. "But know this: we will win in the end. Nathan Bannister can't stand against us, not alone. It's as foolish as a puddle attacking the ocean."

"Nate's not alone," I said. "He has me. And Bosper."

"A girl and a talking dog," he said. "Your forces are formidable." He turned to the others and laughed. They laughed along with him. Even Luria.

"He's only going to get smarter, you know," I told them. "Nate's already smarter than all of you put together, and his intelligence is just going to grow, and—"

"One man cannot stand against the many!" Maculte yelled. "We are *thousands*! He is *one*! If he wants to survive, if *you* want to survive, your only hope is to join us!"

He said a lot of other crazy things, getting madder and madder, until he was fully ranting like some of the people you see on street corners, the ones whose minds have been unhinged for some reason. My brother Steve always laughs at people like that, but I feel sorry for them. I didn't feel sorry for Maculte, though, because he was talking about world conquest, and the destruction

235

of cities, and how "inferior minds" should *welcome* being enslaved, serving their betters, and how if Nate's foolish experiments didn't destroy him then the Red Death Tea Society would certainly do the job, and he kept threatening me, and the pigeons were landing on the ledges again, now staring down at Luria and the men in the red suits, listening to them, and I could see in their eyes that even the pigeons were smart enough to know evil when they saw it.

Maculte was so angry. So very, very angry.

All of them. All the members of the Red Death Tea Society were so very angry, staring up at me.

Which is why they forgot about Proton.

I suppose, in their defense, they weren't wearing the special goggles Nate had made, the ones that allowed me to see Proton. To the assassins, the cat was invisible.

One giant paw came down on their middle car. It crunched.

Proton skidded a bit, trying to find traction, and was obviously quite irritated by this new development. He swatted the other two cars aside, and the members of the Red Death Tea Society went scrambling away, running for their lives and frantically trying to find someplace to hide, which is not that easy to do when you're wearing a bright red suit.

"Ahhhh!" one of them screamed.

"Run!" two of the others yelled.

"My tea!" Luria wailed.

"This isn't over, Delphine Cooper," Maculte hissed, hurrying off down the sidewalk. I have to say, considering that they were an evil organization of assassins, it was funny watching them run for their lives. Or at least it was funnier than when they'd been about to make me . . . gone.

So I laughed.

And the giant cat turned to me.

Proton's eyes narrowed.

"Mwrrr," he said, which I took to mean, "Oh, hello, Delphine. I almost forgot about you, but now let's get back to the clawing and the biting."

He leaped for me.

I dodged.

And the chase was on again.

We were zooming and leaping through the streets. He was snarling. I was loudly explaining that I am far too chewy and absolutely too bony to be tasty. Undaunted by this, Proton was coming closer and closer. His enormous claws were smacking and shredding the pavement with every step, leap, or pounce that he took, sending sparks flying up all around. My belt was sputtering, the rockets misfiring. Proton kept trying to swat me to the ground, and he was only missing by a couple of yards, or only a single yard, or only a measly foot, or even mere inches, with the fur of his leg brushing against me on a couple of occasions, smearing peanut butter off onto my arm. I was twisting through the city streets, looking for any place to hide or any open window I could fly through, or, I don't know, a giant dog that would come to my rescue.

But there wasn't any place to hide and I couldn't quit dodging long enough to look for an open window, and not only were there no giant dogs, I'd left Bosper and Nate far behind, so I was on my own. I'd managed to reach Plove Park, where at least Proton wasn't destroying the city. He could only destroy the grass, the trees, a few park benches, and, well . . .

Me.

My rocket belt quit. Entirely. At the very end it wasn't doing much more than helping me to run really fast, but then it made a *blrrrrkkkk* noise and completely gave up. The smell of a fire momentarily overwhelmed the smell of peanut butter and I realized that the belt had burst into flames, which was unfortunate since I was wearing it. I didn't have time to take it off without becoming a cat toy, so I dived into the creek, scaring a toad that made loud and irritated croaking noises, but I couldn't stay around to apologize or else I would have been making entirely different and far more dire croaking noises of my own. The water put out the fire, but a

giant paw smacked down in the stream next to me, creating a wave that washed me a few yards down the creek, and I scrambled out just in time to see another paw come slicing down and it came so close . . .

. . . that it tore off my goggles.

I was blind.

Well, I wasn't *blind*, but I certainly couldn't see the invisible giant cat. There wasn't anything to do but run (which had been my plan, anyway) and I headed for the woods, running as fast as I could, weaving around so my path wouldn't be quite so predictable, and trying to stay on my feet despite how the ground was rumbling and shaking with every step of the monster cat in pursuit.

Proton was making *rwwerrr* noises and birds were scared up out of the trees and the smell of peanut butter was everywhere and a picnic table just to my right side suddenly crumpled and then I was in the woods.

The trees started smashing all around me. Uprooted. Knocked over. Broken in half. Shattered. They were splintering into bits and pieces. I was running, desperately hurtling through the woods, looking for anywhere to hide, but there is nowhere to hide from a monster cat.

That's why they're monsters.

I was exhausted. I was heaving and huffing and puffing. Scraped and bruised. There was nowhere to run. There was nothing to do.

The cat was going to get me.

And that's when I saw Nate.

He was standing in the woods ahead of me. He smiled when he saw me. I smiled, too. I felt warm. I summoned my last remaining burst of speed, and I ran to him.

"How'd you know I'd be here?" I asked.

"The math was fairly simple," he said. "I knew exactly how long the rocket belt could possibly last. And you're the nicest person I've ever met, so I knew that you'd lead Proton somewhere that he wouldn't hurt anyone else. I knew how fast you could run, and a few other factors and, well, this is where I knew you would be."

"And you have a plan, right? What do we do?" The

noises of the monster coming through the forest were getting louder. Trees were crashing to the ground only fifty feet away.

"No plan," Nate said.

"No plan! Then why did you come here?"

Nate gave me a smile. I'm going to once again point out that Nate and I are not dating, but . . . it was a very nice smile.

He said, "I came here because all of this is my fault. So, I had to come here. I couldn't let you be alone." He reached out and took my hand.

He said, "I guess I wanted to be with you."

I said, "Oh."

Together, holding hands, we faced the oncoming monster. Nate's hand felt comforting in mine. I was entirely happy that he'd finally learned to toss science aside and act from nothing but pure friendship, though I admit I was somewhat disturbed that his victory would be interrupted when we were both stomped into the shape of a cat's paw. The trees were erupting and splintering all around. Wooden shards were flying everywhere. It sounded like the end of the world. I supposed it was, for us. Even holding on to Nate, I almost fell over when the ground seemed to jump beneath our feet, victim of the impact of a towering oak that was brushed aside by Proton's enormous body. Without my goggles, I could barely see him. Just a vague outline of orange and white among the trees. Leaves were falling like rain, knocked from their branches, which were themselves smashing down like hail. Nate hugged me closer, trying to protect me from everything, but it was hopeless. Proton's enormous eyes were looking down from above, fixated on us. His building-size body was drawing breaths that swirled the falling leaves like a small tornado, and one of his paws was raised to . . .

"Hey," I said. "How come I can see him?"

"Huh?" Nate said. "You can?" He hurriedly ripped off his own goggles and tossed them to the ground.

"I can see him, too!" he said.

"But . . . he's invisible, right?"

"Not if the peanut butter is working! Look!" Nate pointed at the giant cat, whose face had suddenly taken on an expression of . . . nausea? And there was a weird *gluung-glunng-gluung* noise coming from him, and Nate's finger, pointing at Proton's face, was angled to a spot that was thirty feet in the air, then twenty-five feet, then twenty.

The cat was suddenly shrinking.

Down to fifteen feet.

Ten.

Five.

Four.

And then . . .

. . . just a regular cat.

"Meeow?" Proton said, looking at me with a dumb-founded expression, then beginning to lick peanut butter off his fur in an entirely innocent manner.

Innocent?

*Hardly.*

"Bad kitty!" I yelled, so loud that it startled Nate and sent the birds (who had just landed again in the trees) once more fluttering into the sky. My yell was so loud that it knocked more leaves from branches and sent Proton skittering away from us, running for safety.

No way.

*No way* that was going to happen.

I was after him in a second, and just as he was trying to leap over a fallen tree, I had him by the scruff of his neck and I plucked him up into the air. He twisted in my grasp, flexed his claws, and was just about to scratch my arms.

"I wouldn't do that," I said. I think ice cubes probably fell from my mouth. My voice was that cold.

"Rwwwr?" Proton said, then slowly retracted his claws and hung limp in my grasp. He was covered, of course, in peanut butter.

I was going to enjoy giving the cat a bath.

Cats *hate* baths.

It was going to take *hours.*

## chapter 12

W hat's that?" Mom asked. "Are you covered in mud?"

"Nope," I said. "Peanut butter." It was all over me, compliments of not only when I'd been spreading it on Proton, but from when he'd been attacking me, and also from when I'd been happily giving the passionately protesting cat a bath for almost an hour before I'd had to leave the rest to Nate and rush home for supper. It had been a reluctant departure on my part, because Proton *deserved* that bath, but even with Betsy roaring along the city streets at full speed I'd barely made it home in time for dinner, sliding into my seat in a frantic dash, because if I'm late for dinner I have to answer questions about *why* I'm late for dinner, and it's awkward to tell your parents that you've been fighting a giant monster. Of course, it's also somewhat

awkward to be a four-feet seven-inch peanut butter dispenser.

There were stares from my family. Various expressions. Mom was scooping mashed potatoes onto her plate, and Steve was staring at me like I was a particularly mystifying alien. Dad, meanwhile, was wiping down the lemonade pitcher because someone had gotten peanut butter all over the handle.

"How did you get that much peanut butter on you?" Mom asked.

"Umm," I said.

"Couldn't you wash up before coming to the table?" Dad asked. He'd moved on from the lemonade pitcher and was wiping up the various other places I'd accidentally spread peanut butter. There were several. In fact, there were multiples of several.

"Umm," I said.

"It's all over your hair," Steve said. "Looks better than usual."

"Piffle," I said.

"Seriously," Mom said, taking a watermelon seed from her mouth, "explain the peanut butter."

"School project," I said. "With Liz. We were making a sand castle, except from peanut butter." You will note that this is not a clever story. Betsy had dropped me off in front of my house and I'd had the entire ride to come up with a plausible story, but I'd instead spent the time thinking happily about how *mad* Proton had been when we'd dumped him in the bath. I do *not* feel that time was wasted, but maybe I could have spared a moment to think up a better excuse for what I'd been doing than making a *peanut-butter sand castle*? It couldn't have taken long.

"You have the strangest school projects," Dad said. "When I was in school all we did was write papers." He had the slightest of grins, as if he knew I was fibbing but was okay with me keeping my secrets. I should mention that, at times, I think Dad is secretly proud of my reputation as a troublemaker. He always encourages me to be active, and he didn't . . . for instance . . . get especially mad the time I tried to build a fort on our roof, or the time Liz and I attached a model rocket to a rope we'd strung all through the house to see if we could get it to travel along the rope like a train track, even though that had resulted in several dents in the walls and also on Steve's leg, and what some people might call a fire on the couch.

"Don't encourage her," Mom told Dad. But she had a smile, too.

Dad said, "Of course not," but he gave me a wink as he cleaned some peanut butter from the saltshaker.

*Beep.*

It was a text from Nate. It said, Thought you might like to see this. There was an image of Proton, being washed.

That cat looked SO mad.

THANK YOU! I texted back.

Speaking of being washed, if you ever find yourself covered in peanut butter, a bath is no good. I speak from experience. Sticky, sopping experience. Also, if you're ever relaxing in the bath, it can be frightening to have a robotic seagull suddenly fly in through the open window. I speak from experience. Shrieking, water-splashing experience.

Luckily, there was a reason for Sir William to come flying in through the window. He was bringing me a ray gun built from a hair dryer, an invention of Nate's that disintegrated peanut butter.

There was a note from Nate, telling me about the ray gun, and adding,

*I just invented this. I thought you might need it to get rid of all the peanut butter. A bath is no good. I speak from experience.*

After dinner, after my bath, after using the ray gun to disintegrate the peanut butter, and after hurriedly hiding Sir William when Steve almost caught me carrying the robotic seagull down the hallway, I went around to all my friends' houses and made sure they didn't drink any of the strange tea that had shown up on their doorsteps—the tea that had been delivered with cards saying it was from me—even though Nate had assured me the tea was safe.

It's not that I didn't trust Nate, it's just that the tea *was* from the Red Death Tea Society and I don't trust a secret organization of power-hungry assassins with anything, not even tea.

So I nabbed the tea from Stine Keykendall, and Ventura León, and from my homeroom teacher, Mrs. Isaacson, who invited me inside her house to look at her paintings, because she knows my mom is an art agent and I think she was trying to hint that my mom should represent her, but the paintings were all of cats and even though they were pretty good they were making me shiver and it wasn't the best time to show them to me.

I also gathered the Red Death Tea Society tea from my mom, and from Steve (I had Sir William waddle into his room and nab it), and a few others, but failed to get it back from Tommy Brilp, who came to his door actually drinking a cup of it, *assuring* me he was drinking a cup of it, and wanting to know if I would go to the movies with him on Monday. Or . . . Tuesday? Possibly Wednesday or Thursday? Or Friday or Saturday or Sunday or any other day of the week, even though I was pretty sure he'd mentioned them all.

I said, "Sorry, can't. I'm grounded," which is an excuse I frequently use, because it's quite believable.

Back home, I buried all the tea I'd gathered in my backyard. Deep. In plastic bags, with warnings written on them.

*Beep.*

It was another text from Nate. I was stretched out in bed, back in my normal world, with Steve playing music too loud from his room.

The text said, This peanut butter is really a mess. Had to shave off some of Proton's hair. There was an image of a partially shaved, snarling Proton.

KEEP SENDING THESE TEXTS, I wrote back.

*Beep.*

It was a text from Liz.

This is my eyeball, it said.

There was a close-up picture of her eyeball.

Right before bed, I went down to the kitchen to get a glass of water. Dad was watching the news in the living room. It was scenes of downtown Polt. Crushed cars. Partially collapsed buildings. That sort of thing.

"Did you hear about this?" Dad said, gesturing to the television. "Some sort of unknown cause, but a lot of property damage."

"Oh," I said. "Uhh. Hmm. Ahhh." It was not my smoothest moment.

"Best guess for the cause is some sort of abnormal weather system. Maybe a small tornado. Basically, a freak storm."

"Hmm," I said, walking off. I didn't want to say anything, because if I didn't say anything then I wasn't technically lying by not telling Dad that it wasn't a freak storm that had caused all the damage.

It was a freak feline.

*Beep.*

It was another text from Liz.

This is my other eyeball, it said.

There was a close-up picture of her other eyeball.

I fluffed my pillow.

Twice.

I couldn't sleep.

It felt so weird to be in my normal room at the end of such an extraordinary day. It felt like something else was going to happen. My thoughts were racing about. It felt like I was shivering with energy. It felt like my room was smaller than ever before. The moon felt bright. Snarls, Mom's cat, padded along the hallway outside my door, and made a meowing sound. I got up and made sure my door was closed, because, duh . . . cat. When I was walking back to my bed my phone beeped, and for one second I worried that it was Snarls texting me. But it was Nate.

I can't sleep, he wrote. And I've calculated a 98.94% chance that you can't either.

Make that 100%, I texted back.

I'm sorry about getting you involved with the Red Death Tea Society, he wrote. There was a picture of Maculte. Nate had given him donkey ears.

It happens, I texted back, although of course it does not, as a general rule, happen.

I'm glad we didn't die, Nate wrote. There was a picture of his hand giving a thumbs-up.

Me too, I said.

I'm glad we're friends, Nate wrote.

Me too, I said.

I think I can sleep now, Nate wrote. There was a picture of a pillow.

Me too, I wrote back. I put my phone on my nightstand, fluffed my pillow, smiled, and was asleep in moments.

# chapter 13

You might think that Nate and I grew close after that, hanging out together all the time. You'd be wrong. We only went on with our normal lives, the day-to-day schoolwork, with me walking the dogs and joining the soccer team, and Nate . . . ? Well, for a genius like Nate, there are always projects to work on (I saw him late one night on the football field, testing a spray gun that shot peanut butter), and frankly I'm not sure that Nate's concept of time was the same as mine, or anyone else's.

We texted back and forth a few times, but it was harder to talk in person. I think Nate was embarrassed about losing control of his experiment, or about almost getting us killed, and it was one of those times when a silence builds until it almost feels like a wall.

Time passed.

The days added up.

Weeks went by.

I would see Nate in class, of course. He always sat near the front (I usually gravitate toward the back, where the occasional misbehavior is not as readily caught), and I noticed how most of my classmates ignored him. He wasn't invited to parties. Wasn't picked to be on any teams in gym class. Nobody hung out at his locker. Nobody sat with him during lunch.

Nobody thought he was amazing.

He just moved through the halls and the classrooms, unnoticed.

Well, *I* thought he was amazing.

We would wave hello in the halls. He held a door for me a couple of times. We would wave hello in the lunch-room. I held a door for him a couple of times. Liz and Stine kept asking why I was so obviously interested in Nate, and why I wasn't *talking* to him if I *was* so interested. What I wanted to tell them was everything that had happened with Proton and the Red Death Tea Society and with Nate, but I didn't. It never seemed right to tell them. It seemed like it was a shared secret between Nate and me, except that even we weren't sharing the secret.

Not anymore.

What I wanted most of all was to tell Nate that I'd

spent an entire night packing a duffel bag full of items I thought might be needed on our next adventure, because surely there *would* be a next adventure, right?

*Right?*

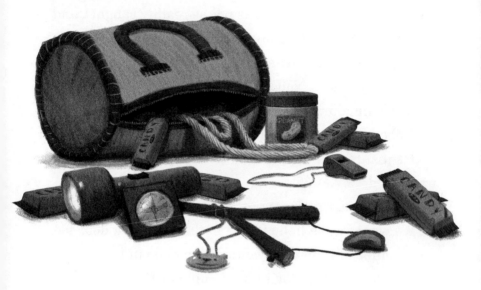

But the days and the weeks went by, and my bag was just tucked beneath my bed. Gathering dust. Full of rope. Slingshots. Peanut butter. My sturdiest shoes. A first-aid kit. More candy bars than I will admit. A good-luck charm that I decided to keep, even though it's shaped like a cat. A lighter. A compass. A whistle. A flashlight with extra batteries. And so on, and so on.

I played a lot of soccer.

I thought about cats and rocket belts, and about the Red Death Tea Society and how they had interfered with Nate's experiment, and how they'd attacked me, and what they might do next. It didn't feel like anything was finished. I knew they were out there. Planning. I thought about what Maculte had said about Nate being alone. And he *was* alone. And it wasn't right. And, for the first time in my life I felt alone, too. I was still seeing all my friends, still hanging out with Liz, still being the person I used to be, but without Nate I still felt alone.

I found myself being suspicious of any black cars, of which I saw hundreds, but nothing ever came of it. I thought I saw Maculte in one of the cars, but it drove away before I could be sure.

I didn't feel like I was sure of anything.

Not anything.

I made extra money at my dog-walking job and I spent it on science books because . . . I don't know. I just did.

Liz Morris and I went camping one weekend with her parents.

I thought about forming a band.

I began to think that Nate and I weren't going to be friends after all.

I read a lot of books, not only the science books but others with Sherlock Holmes, or the heroes and gods of ancient Greece, who seemed to spend the majority of their time making up for horrible mistakes. I was jealous of them: making mistakes is bad, but . . . at least they were doing *something*.

I was outside in my yard on Friday the thirteenth when the call came. I was drinking lemonade and wondering if I'd put in too much sugar. I was deciding that I had, and was also deciding that I was okay with that. I was devising my own little stories wherein Sherlock Holmes was hired to solve the mysteries of the Greek gods, and I was also watching Snarls, our cat, walking across the lawn. I was keeping a close eye on him, because I no longer entirely trusted cats.

His ears perked up.

He heard my phone before I did.

I picked up my phone and looked to see who was calling.

Nate.

It was Nate.

I'll be honest and admit that I started to sweat. But I answered right away.

"Hello?" I said. "Nate?"

"Delphine?" he said. "I need your help. Could you come over? I've done something not-so-very smart."

By then I'd spilled lemonade all over my lawn, and I was inside my room and clutching my adventure bag in my hands.

"I'll be right there," I told him.

# Acknowledgments

A big thanks to Colleen Coover, my first reader and the one person who always thinks I'm a genius, even when I'm having trouble figuring out the curtains or how to make soup. Big thanks also to Joanna Volpe at New Leaf Literary & Media, whose advice was the first step in getting this book on the shelves. And to my agent, Brooks Sherman at the Bent Agency, the guy who took a look at the first glowing goop of this novel and decided there was something there, and then kindly used his cattle prod on the lowest setting in order to cajole me into doing the necessary revisions. Huge thanks to Cindy Loh and everyone else at Bloomsbury, because you people took a chance on me and have been unfailingly supportive and generous with your time and expertise. This would be a far lesser book without all your efforts.

I'd also like to give a rousing cheer for Thierry Lafontaine for his amazing illustrations. After having written so much about these characters, it was wonderful to "see" them for the first time. Thanks to my mom and dad, for understanding that it would have done little good to punish me for all my various transgressions, and that sometimes you just have to let a little boy get bumped and bruised and . . . at one point . . . somehow manage to get his mouth chock-full of angry bumblebees. Thanks also to everyone who puts up with all the questions I ask, and thanks to people like Neil DeGrasse Tyson, Richard Feynman, and Carl Sagan, who provided some of the answers.

**260**